WHEEL C

BOO

the
queen
of witches

BRANDI ELLEDGE

Printed by Aelurus Publishing, March 2019

Cover design by Molly Phipps

ISBN 13: 978-1-912775-09-5

www.aeluruspublishing.com

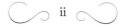

dedication

To Matt,

You might not have a gallant steed or shiny armor but you're still my knight. And you're the best dang knight the South has ever seen.

acknowledgements

There were a lot of great people that helped with this book. My savvy editor, Rebecca Jaycox; the amazing Aelurus Publishing team; Jeff and his fantastic proofreader Katherine. A million thanks to you three for getting this book to where it needed to be.

Special thanks to my husband for the endless coffee runs and my two sweet kids that ask me every day, "How many words did you get today, mama?"

To my own mother, you are literally the strongest person I've ever known. I love you big. Also, thanks for listening to me drone on and on about my characters and enjoying them as much as I do. And to my witty, amazing, funny dad...psych! I had you going there for a second, didn't I? I told you old man you must wait until book five. Big hugs for the rest of the good looking members of my crazy family who've cheered me on from the sidelines. Big thanks to God for giving me these said crazy family members.

An eerie quiet settled over the forest. It was almost as if nature knew something wasn't right with me either and it was scared. Louisiana was full of wildlife, from considerable predators to pesky mosquitoes, and yet nothing made a sound. Nothing. Nada. Zilch. But to be fair, I was a little afraid of myself.

There always had been something different… a little bit off about me, but here recently, I was getting worse. This thing inside gnawing at me wanted to be released, and sometimes I could barely contain what I had been referring to as "the disease," because how else would I label it?

I had told no one other than my best friend about my disease, or the turmoil I was going through. The loneliness I feel is never-ending. But I must keep this a secret. If people found out about me, they might harm me or send me off to a government lab as a scientific experiment. People tended to shy away from the abnormal. I had asked my bestie to meet me out in the woods behind our school for a little pow-wow, knowing that if we were caught, we would get detention. I'd reiterated she would have to be quiet, and she promised me stealth was her middle name. I listened as my friend crashed through the woods, cringing as sticks snapped and curse words were muttered. That girl could wake the living dead. We were so going to get caught.

Blonde hair came into my peripheral vision. "Ugh! How many times have I told you, Charlie, that I don't do the great outdoors. This is so beneath me."

We might have been best friends since kindergarten, but some things never changed. I sat down on a fallen log and looked at my friend as she walked through the woods towards me. She tiptoed on the fallen leaves, trying her hardest not to ruin her designer shoes while her eyes darted everywhere but at me. Like she was preparing for an alligator to surprise attack her.

"Tandi, we are literally in the woods right behind our school. The swamp is miles away from here. The chances of you getting mauled by an alligator are slim to none."

"Do I look like I give a rat's ass about percentages? Besides, I am always in the three percentile, so the odds are already against me."

Tandi looked exactly like a chubbier version of Ashley Benson from the television show Pretty Little Liars. She hated being plump, but what she never seemed to notice was she was beautiful. Not just pretty or cute, but stunningly beautiful. But because of her skirt size, she disagreed. That was an argument for another day, though. She bit her full lip, glancing at where I sat. After rolling my eyes, I took off my flannel shirt, leaving me in just a ribbed tank top. I spread out the flannel shirt on the log for her.

"Oh, thank the Lord." She sat down on my shirt. "I mean, these pants do cost more than I would like to admit. And why the heck are we meeting out here? When I received your text, I almost ignored it, but then I thought if you do go over the edge into crazyville, I want you on my side."

"Hardy, har, har." I couldn't deny it. I did feel like I was on the cusp of something. Teetering on the edge of sanity and batshit crazy. "I brought you out here because I wanted to tell you something."

Her perfect eyebrows lifted. "I swear to you right now, if you start chanting demonic crap while your head spins, I'm outta here."

"What's happening to me is not funny." I brushed a tear from my eye, as she threw an arm around me. Neither of us said anything for a few seconds. "Last night, I was in my room going through an old family photo album. At first, I cried buckets of tears, and then I was angry—angry at the person who took my parents from me. The album caught fire in my hands. The front and back of the book was completely burnt, along with some of the pictures. I was able to put the fire out¬—but still! What am I going to do? Ever since I turned eighteen it's getting worse!"

Tandi rubbed my back. "Can you try to show me?"

"You know it doesn't work like that. That is why it's so scary. What if that happens during school? Or worse, what if I hurt someone? I have to find a cure."

"I get why you're upset, and I don't want you to think I am making light of the situation, but maybe you're looking at this all wrong. Maybe it's not a disease. Maybe it's a gift."

"You know dang well that's a lie. Wondering if you might accidentally turn your teacher into ash is not a gift."

Her nose twitched. "It depends. Which teacher are we talking about? Mrs. Morris? Because if so, good riddance. I hate that woman."

I half cried and half laughed. "I don't know what I'm going to do."

"You are going to keep putting one foot in front of the other until we can figure this whole thing out. It sounds like you were having strong emotions when you torched the family album, so try and stay calm and stay away from Brandon."

Brandon was my ex-boyfriend as of yesterday. He wanted to take our relationship to the next level, and when I refused, he got extremely angry with me. That's when I decided to end things. I had enough on my plate without having to deal with a pushy, volatile boyfriend.

Tandi was scowling, which meant she was thinking about how I ended it with Brandon, too. "You really should talk with your brother. Wes might be able to help you." I shook my head and Tandi sighed. "So I've got good news and better news. The good news is lunch break is over, and we can no longer hide out in this barbarous place."

"The woods?"

She shrugged. "You say woods; I say serial killer's paradise. And the better news is we have a new student. Girl, he is so fine. I didn't catch his name because I was too busy staring at his beautiful face. I mean, seriously, he should take insurance out on that thing. What if he was to get in an accident? Talk about a tragedy. I don't know his name, so I've dubbed him 'face' because let's be honest, his real name isn't the important part."

I was laughing as I stood. She threw her arm around me as we headed back to our small school that was ideal for the wealthy patrons of Peu Blue, Louisiana. Unlike Tandi, I was far from wealthy, but my parents had left my brother and me some money. The money from their will allowed us to pay the mortgage on the house and my tuition to attend Peu Blue Academy. Since Wes my brother graduated two years ago, he had started to make a name for himself. His love for painting was finally paying off. Of course, that meant he was away from home more nights than I would like, but he was making money and following his dream, so I was proud of him. Tandi believed I should talk with my brother about what I'm going through, but I couldn't put this burden on him.

We'd lost our parents twenty-three months ago, so at the age of eighteen, Wes became my guardian. He had to figure out how to manage the money our parents left us: paying off the house, the car, and making sure there was enough money for tuition, so I could graduate with my friends. He gave up going to college to help raise me and now he was finally carving out some time for him and his painting. No, I couldn't go to him with this.

I had my head down, thinking about my life, while Tandi talked non-stop about some new shop that just opened up, when I ran into someone. His arms reached out to steady me. I looked up to see who I almost plowed over. This must be the new kid. Dark auburn hair was swooped to one side, and warm brown eyes stared down at me. He was two inches taller than me, so he was around five feet nine. He had a prominent dimple in his chin that just added to his good looks.

Tandi threw both hands up in the air. "I knew you should have got insurance. Tell me," she said, as her thumb hitched in my direction, "did this twat hurt your face?"

The new kid looked at my friend oddly. "No. I think we're good."

The school bell was ringing. Lunch was officially over, and I really needed to get to my next class. Mr. Hawking hated tardiness.

"Do you need help getting to your next class?" I didn't want to be rude to the new kid, but he just stood there in front of me with a bashful grin on his charming face. He was borderline gawking, and I had places to be. "Tandi here could show you where to go."

He ran a hand over his face. "I'm staring. Sorry. It's just you know… you're beautiful." I gave Tandi a what-the-hell look. The new kid was cute but awkward. "Pardon me. I shouldn't have said that out loud. I'm Talon."

He was hot. I'd give him that, but something in the way his eyes roamed my face made me feel uncomfortable. And not just because I was a virgin, and he was looking at me like he was thirsty, and I was the last drop of water on the planet.

"Um, cool. Nice to me you, Talon. I'm Charlize. Charlie to my friends and I'm also late to class, so if you'll excuse me."

As I sidestepped him, I didn't have to look over my shoulder to know Tandi was rolling her eyes. Didn't care. I had bigger problems.

Our small private school appeared more like a fire station with its one-story, red brick layout and gigantic windows. Our school wasn't dilapidated but by no means was it fancy. Come to think of it I wasn't sure where all of the tuition went to. Maybe in the new headmaster's bank account. He did have a sweet ride. I studied the creaky old building and caught my teacher through the far window on the left, glaring at me. His nose was almost against the window pane as he watched me walk into the school. So much for giving him the excuse that I was in the little girl's room. Ugh. This day was going to suck.

I was halfway up the brick steps leading to the metal door of our school when the new kid shouted. "Wait!" I tried to curb my aggravation as I turned towards him, giving him my attention. "I know this is very unorthodox, but would you like to go on a date with me tonight?"

"I'm sorry but—"

Tandi interrupted me. "Of course, she can, but she'll have to take her own car and meet you in a well-lit public place because I watch Date Line, and even though your face is amazing, I don't trust it."

I didn't know what to say, because, really, where does one go from here? "Talon, thank you for the offer, but I really have a ton of studying to do before Christmas break."

He sauntered up the steps toward me. I know his slow walk was supposed to be sexy, and I could hear a couple of appreciative girls who were also running late for class sighing, but since I had already determined there was something wrong with me, I didn't feel bad for losing my patience.

He finally reached me, and I was beyond annoyed. I crossed my arms and all but tapped my foot on the brick steps. He gave me a disarming smile before he leaned down, putting his lips against my ears as he whispered, "Why are you living here, amongst humans, when you were meant for so much more? Meet me at the diner after school, and I'll answer all of your questions."

I stood there in shock as he walked away. What did he mean "amongst humans" and what exactly was I meant for? Did the new kid know what was wrong with me? My stomach knotted with tension and I felt like I was about to throw up.

Tandi was beside me in mere seconds. "You're completely pale. What did that jerk say to you?"

"He implied that I might not be human, and he could answer my questions."

We stood there for several minutes in silence. Neither of us cared that we were incredibly late at this point.

"Well, we have two options," Tandi said. "We can blow this joint and head to Mexico, or we can both go to the diner after school and see what he has to say. Not human?" She snorted. "What are you, an alien? And if so, can we make money off of this?"

I rolled my eyes so hard I thought they were going to fall out of my head. I couldn't care less about school at the moment, but if I didn't show up for a class, my brother would get an automated phone call. I definitely didn't need him asking any questions right now. Especially, since I had no answers. We headed to our classes, and the rest of the day I was in zombie mode. I could only think about the new kid, Talon, and if he really did know what was wrong with me.

chapter two

W e were in a booth at Ma's Diner, and I glared at Tandi in disbelief, as she sat across from me cool as a cucumber in an array of different shades of pink. Her life's motto was, "It'll either work out or it won't," meanwhile I could have an inch of water in my boat and I would already be planning for the boat to capsize.

Tandi stopped studying her hot pink nail polish to look at me. "Charlie, why are you looking at me like I just ran over your dog?"

"Because I'm nervous, and you won't stop chomping on your gum, and I'm taking out all my anxiety on you. Sound good?"

Tandi shrugged. "Sure. You're never the irrational one, so why not give you a day to act insane? Since you're taking my job today, I'll try to be the sweet, calm, mature one."

"Good luck," I huffed.

The door to the diner swung open and in walked Talon. He came up to our booth and sat down.

"So, we meet again." He nodded at us both. "Do either of you mind if I make this conversation private?"

I glanced at Tandi to see what she thought about his question. "How exactly do you plan to do that?"

He clapped his hands together. The air over our booth turned shimmery. We could see the other customers in the diner, but they were blurry. A waitress started to come to our table, but then she suddenly did an about face, heading in the opposite direction.

"How did you do that?" I asked.

"Power of persuasion." He gave a laugh. "This is nothing compared to what you should be able to do."

"What do you mean? Do you know about... about me?"

Tandi said, "Maybe you shouldn't say anything else, Charlie. Not until we figure out what it is he wants. Because you do want something, don't you?"

Talon briefly dropped his smile. "Actually, yes, I do. I don't have the time to explain who you are or what you can do in full detail, but I would like to offer you a chance of a lifetime. There is a training school not too far from here. We would like to offer you room and board, and after you're done with training, you will be employed with us."

"Sorry. No. You show up out of the blue and seem to know a whole lot about me while I know nothing about you. I'm going to need you to explain things. Let's start with training for what"? I asked. "And I can't just pick up and leave town. I have to finish school. Also, I would have to tell my brother something, and how do I know that this is legit?"

"Your training would help you with your powers. I've read your file. I know that your parents are recently deceased. You need someone to lean on for information. My people can help you do that. Not having anyone show you how to control your powers could be dangerous for you and," he said, glancing at Tandi, "your friends. You can finish out school year at our school for the gifted, and considering that we are offering you a full scholarship, your brother should be happy."

Yeah, but I couldn't talk to my brother about this. "It couldn't wait six months until I graduated from high school?"

He leaned back in his chair. "I'm afraid not. We're going to need to know your answer by the end of the week. Then, unfortunately, the offer will be off the table."

My gut was screaming that what he just said was bullshit. "Call me crazy but I doubt that. Why is this a now or never kind of thing?"

"I honestly can't say until you are at our camp. Right now you're considered an outsider and there is certain information that we can't share with outsiders."

Wasn't that just a tidy answer. "Tell me this then… how did you find me?"

"We have trained professionals that are constantly on the lookout for unfamiliar activity. You are letting out strong power surges in blips here and there, so we knew that a newbie was coming into his or her powers. I've actually been here a week or so looking for who was unleashing the burst of power. Today, I decided to try the private school. After I ran into you earlier, which was pure luck by the way, I requested a file on you." That was a little creepy. Hot guy or not. "You will learn how to control your power during training, and I will be your personal mentor." He checked his watch and then slid a card with his number on it. "You can reach me on my cell at any time. I'm going to let you think about what I've said and when you have more questions, please let me know."

As he stood, I said, "What if I don't want these—powers? What if I wanted to make them go away?"

"Then I could help you with that, too. It would be a shame to let your powers go to waste, but if you decide that this is not the life that you want, then I can make your powers go away. You will be as normal as your friend here."

Tandi threw her long, blonde hair behind her shoulder. "There is nothing about me that is normal."

He gave her smile as he tipped an imaginary hat to both of us. "I'll be waiting on your call, Charlie."

We watched in fascination as the bubble around us disappeared. Tandi waited until Talon had left the diner before she started talking ninety miles per minute.

"Whoa. What are you thinking? Because I'm thinking that this is all just too easy."

I was about to ask her what she meant, but I understood. I had a flaw. You could dress it up and call it powers or even a gift, but at the end of the day, it was still a flaw in my book, and someone just happened to show up and say they could help me solve all my problems. No, I was calling B.S. on that, too.

"You're right; it's too easy."

"I know you're looking for answers but we have to be careful on how we get them."

She was right. I had to be careful that I didn't let the excitement of finding someone—someone like me—be the deciding factor of my future. One that could very well be a bad decision. Like joining a group I knew nothing about, just to feel like I belonged.

Tandi tapped her nails on the table as she mused. "Oh, but that face of his. Yum." She looked around the diner. "Since we're here, we're going to eat, right?"

How she could think about food at a time like this, I had no clue. "Sure. I have nothing else better to do." Other than sitting here and stressing over my life and how some organization apparently has a file on me. They now know enough about me to track me down. That can't be good. The pit in my stomach grew because I wasn't entirely sure that Talon and his organization were the good guys. "I'm going to seriously think about what he said. Maybe there are others out there just like me that could also help." Maybe Talon wasn't my only option.

Tandi's legs shook under the table. She was worried about me. As she sat there gazing out the window, her carefree attitude gone, and in its place was a girl that was afraid. Afraid for her friend. Finally, she spoke. "Charlie, I know you, and I know that whatever is happening to you…" Her voice almost broke. "I know that it's serious. I know that you want—no, need—answers, but I'm asking that you really think about going off alone with some stranger just because he says he can help you."

I knew what she was saying. I needed to do my own research on Talon and who I am. Create my own file. How people could know more about me than I do was unacceptable. I was worried too, but I was out of time. Every morning I woke up, I heard the same thing.

Tick. Tock.

It was just a matter of time before I hurt someone, and what if it was Tandi? I could never live with myself.

"Tandi, everything will be all right." That sounded false, even to my ears.

"We need to talk about this. None of this feels right. Something about Face is just making my Spidey Sense go off."

"I know." A group of football players sat in the booth behind us. I was scared they would overhear our conversation, and that's all I needed. "We can talk about this later, but I know what you mean. I'm not buying what he's selling."

Obviously, Tandi wasn't buying it either. As she signaled the waitress over, she mumbled out of the side of her mouth, "All of this anxiety you've given me is making me extra hungry." Giving me a hopeful look, she added, "We should just run away to some exotic island. Get us a couple of cabana boys to rub hot oil all over us while we watch every show we can find on Netflix."

Before I could tell her that plan couldn't happen for more than one reason, Jenny, one of the two waitresses employed at Ma's Diner, sashayed over to our table, popping her bubble gum. Jenny had a long-standing feud with Tandi. They had hated each other since kindergarten. Jenny was captain of the cheerleading team, and she was also the homecoming queen at our high school. One thing she had perfected over the years was her phony smile, not to mention her knack of putting down others while making it sound like it was just a harmless little joke. Unfortunately, Tandi was usually the butt of Jenny's jokes. The truth was Jenny was jealous of Tandi. Not just because Tandi was prettier, but because Tandi was richer, and that was the one thing Jenny never had. Money. She went to our school on a scholarship and she seemed to be the only one that had a problem with that.

With one last pop of her bubble gum, Jenny took out her pad and pen. "Y'all ready to order?"

There was no need to look at the menu. I had it memorized since I was twelve. "I'll have the special without lettuce, please, and a sweet tea."

Tandi gathered both of our menus and handed them to Jenny. "I'll have the exact same, but with a side order of fried okra, mashed potatoes with gravy, and a hash brown casserole."

Jenny gave Tandi a body scan. "You know, hon, all that extra food will make you fatter."

Tandi gave Jenny the stank eye. "I am a full-figured gal. I. Have. To. Eat. In order to keep my full figure. That's how it works, hon."

"Well, you are what you eat," Jenny said.

Tandi crossed her legs, murmuring, "You must eat a lot of Hot Pockets because they're cheap and easy."

I coughed into my hand to hide my smile. "I think that's it, Jenny. Thanks."

With a little huff, she muttered, "Freaks," under her breath, turning around and heading back to the kitchen where we could hear her calling our order out.

"Did she just call us freaks? Finally, hanging out with you has given me the bad reputation I always wanted." I laughed, and she asked, "Do you believe the nerve of some people? Maybe you should go to training. Learn how to wield these so-called powers that Talon said you

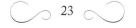

have. What are the freaky things you've said you can do so far?" She held up her hand and started listing things on her fingers. "You made fog swirl around us that one time you fell asleep at my house. Then there was the time you turned your coffee to ice. You found that lost kid pretty quickly. But none of those are going to work for me. Oh! I know, you set fire to a photo album. That one. I'll take that one." She pointed a finger to Jenny. "Make her catch on fire."

Smiling, I shook my head. Out of all the best friends in the world and I landed this one. I was one lucky girl. "Ever since my eighteenth birthday three months ago, you have been handling all of these incidents so well. Way better than me. I'm impressed."

Her green eyes rolled. "So, I'm guessing that you're not going to make a bonfire out of Jenny?"

"Stop! Here she comes."

Jenny came back over with our sweet teas, putting them down on the table a little harder than she should have and walked off to another table.

Tandi took a sip of tea, then leaned in close to me. "Have you told your brother yet about your little secret?"

I looked around the diner to make sure no one was paying attention to us. "No, I haven't. I think that's a discussion for down the road. When he's rich and famous and has fulfilled his dreams of becoming a successful painter."

Tandi smirked. "That boy could make millions being a model. I used to have the hots for him until I saw him in his Captain America underwear."

"Tandi! He was seven." I was laughing as I excused myself. "I'm going to the ladies' room. Be back in a sec. Don't you dare get into it with Jenny before I get back, all right?"

Tandi fluffed her hair. "You scared I'll hurt the little trollop?"

Sliding out of the booth, I grinned over my shoulder. "No, I'm scared I'll miss out on the action."

I said a little prayer that Jenny wouldn't purposely drop our food on the floor before serving it to us, as I weaved my way to the back of the crowded diner before turning left down the narrow hallway. My stomach clenched at the thought of leaving my home, Tandi, and not finishing out my senior year of high-school. What else was I supposed to do? Head down and lost in thought, I smacked into some poor soul. Ugh! How many people could I possibly run over in one day? I was on a roll. I was already offering up apologies as warm hands grabbed me by my shoulders, helping me to stay on my feet. My teeth clenched as I felt sharp jolts go up my arms, almost leaving a numbing sensation in their wake. Shocked, I jerked back, breaking contact with the energy pumping into my body. I gazed into the face of my discomfort.

He was an angel. I mean, there were no wings or halo, but hot damn boy! He had blond, shaggy hair, electric blue eyes, and stubble that couldn't hide his perfect cheekbones. More than six feet tall, he was built like a running back. He stood in front of me, shaking his head like he was confused, so I started to reach out and touch him, but thought better of it. I didn't want to get another shock.

The silence in the hallway bordered on awkward, and I was slightly embarrassed I hadn't watched where I was going when I plowed right into this stranger. He stared at me like I had two heads. Probably because I had all but drooled over him. A little unnerved, I mumbled, "Excuse me," and went to sidestep him.

Like it was a dance, he stepped with me, so he was right back in front of me, blocking me from the bathrooms. He cleared his throat. "I'm sorry. You're not hurt, are you?"

"No." I peered up into his blue eyes and almost lost my train of thought, causing my next words to come out in a rush. "It's my fault. I was lost in thought and not paying attention to where I was going, and, well, then you happened."

"Then I happened." He gave me a wolfish smile. "Are you from here?"

"Yes. Born and raised. But if you were from here, you would know that because there's a population of around eight thousand." My eyes causally roamed over his body. "We don't get many visitors out this way, and most people would never intentionally move to this small town, because it is super expensive to live in." I put a strand of hair behind my ear, a nervous habit of mine. "Not that this isn't a nice town or the people aren't friendly, 'cause we are, it's just that there isn't enough work here in our small town. It's mostly a retirement community." It took everything I had not to cringe. Never in my life had I ever been so rattled. "So, are you visiting someone or lost?"

"Neither." His smile was brief. "It's more like business brought me here."

Narrowing my eyes in disbelief, I asked, "Business brought you to this town?"

"Yes, and it looks as if it's not as cut and dry as I'd initially hoped for, so I guess I'll be staying for a while. Can you tell me where the nearest hotel is?"

"There's a bed-and-breakfast one road over from main street." Almost apologetic, I added, "Since we don't get many out-of-towners this way, it's the only place in town we have to offer visitors."

"As long as it has warm water and a phone, it'll be perfect. I lost my cell phone somewhere in South America and haven't had a chance to get a new one yet. I have an older brother who I'm sure is probably panicking, because I haven't checked in with him in about four weeks."

I gave him a small smile. "Well, my best friend would have died without her cell phone for four weeks, so I commend you." I reached into my back pocket and pulled out my cell and handed it to him, careful not to touch him in the process. "Gretchen, the owner of the bed-and-breakfast, will charge you an arm and a leg if your call isn't local, so if you want, you can use my cell phone while I'm in the bathroom."

His smile was so bright it made me feel like I just gave him a kidney transplant instead of my phone. "That must be a Southern thing? Usually, people aren't so trusting."

My eyebrows rose. "Are you planning on stealing my phone?"

"I can swear to you that no harm will come to your phone while in my possession." He tapped my phone on his palm. "Thanks. I'll stay right here, and I'll be done by the time you get out."

I stepped around him, and this time he let me pass. "You don't have to hurry. I've got an older brother myself, and I know how they can be."

I had one hand on the bathroom doorknob when he said, "Hey, I'm Jamison by the way. What's your name?"

"Charlize." Turning back, I grinned. "But my friends call me Charlie."

As I entered the bathroom, I heard the mysterious Jamison say, "Pleasure to meet you, beautiful."

chapter three

olling my eyes as the door closed behind me, I let out a girly sigh. Of course, something that hot had a book full of pretty lines for the ladies. With compliments like that, I bet he had tons of girls falling at his feet. But not this girl. No, sir. After dating a controlling boyfriend for the better part of a year, I'd decided to keep boys at an arm's length. If Tandi thought Talon was hot, I couldn't wait for her to catch a glimpse of the angel.

I stared at my reflection above the tiny, grungy sink. Dark, brown hair grazed the tops of my shoulders and dazed, long-lashed violet eyes stared back at me. Tandi said I had an uncanny resemblance to Vivien Leigh, which was what made her befriend me in Miss Jones's class. She had an obsession with Southern movies, and Gone with the Wind was like the Holy Grail to her. That and Steel Magnolias, with Fried Green Tomatoes coming in third.

I washed my hands and headed out of the restroom. Jamison was still in the dark hallway, talking quietly into the phone. I overheard him say, "Yes, that's exactly what I said. It's not my fault that you went all the way to South

America. If my phone hadn't been destroyed, I would have called you and told you not to waste your time." He started pacing then he sighed into the phone. "Define 'demolished.' Listen, not to change the subject, but you know how Ariana said I should take off by myself? It's because South America led me to this little town in Louisiana, where I can find the key. But get this, it's also where my—" The door to the girls' bathroom shut and Jamison swiveled around. "Hey, bro, gotta go. I have to return this cell phone to the beautiful girl I borrowed it from."

I could hear someone on the other line still talking, but Jamison hung up and handed the phone back to me.

"You didn't have to hurry on my account."

He smiled at me. "That's all right. I was done talking."

There were a thousand questions going through my mind like, What key? and What the heck got demolished? But I decided to bite my tongue. Just because he was using my phone, it didn't make it my business.

I needed to get back to my table, but my Southern roots wouldn't allow me just to stroll off without a proper goodbye, so I heard myself spitting out, "Well, it was so nice meeting you, Jamison. I hope you enjoy your stay here in our small town."

He gave me a predatory smile, making me shiver all the way down my spine. Yep, definitely a bad boy. "Oh, I'm sure I'll more than enjoy my stay here."

I turned on my heel and walked as quickly as possible back to the booth.

Tandi was scrolling through her text messages on her phone. Without looking up, she asked, "What in the world took you so long? I told you to quit eating all that fiber. I thought about coming to find you, but someone has to stay out here to make sure Jenny doesn't spit in our food, that un-classy trollop."

Looking over my shoulder, I saw Jamison hop up on a barstool not too far away with his back to me, and I released a little sigh. Tandi drew my attention by making a gurgling sound. There she sat with her jaw open like a bigmouth bass.

I whispered, "You better close that before you catch flies."

Tandi looked at Jamison, then me, and whispered, "Who is that hunk of burning love?"

I explained to her about me literally running into him and our small talk before and after the use of my cell phone.

Her beautiful pouty lips came together in a classic Tandi smirk. "Well, if that's not a sign from God, I don't know what is."

At this point, we were leaning so close to each other our noses were almost touching. "What in the heck are you talking about, Tandi?"

Tandi sighed like I was an idiot. "Duh. You're sitting here contemplating whether you should join some kind of X-Men training camp or not, then that stud muffin comes strolling into town, and the way he keeps glancing over here every once in a while means that the attraction is mutual."

"Listen, first of all, I am not attracted to him, so there is nothing mutual about it." Maybe I was attracted to him, but I wasn't admitting it. "And last but not least, I'm pretty sure he has ties with the mafia. Or maybe he's CIA, FBI, or some other acronym for badasses."

Her eyebrows rose.

"It's true. I heard him on the phone talking about demolishing things in South America."

"Maybe he's a building contractor, and that's his job." She shrugged. "I don't care if he's the head honcho of the largest cartel in the world. It still doesn't cancel his hotness, and you should tag that."

My jaw dropped. "You are a slut, my friend. There will be no tagging of anything. He is not a deer, and my opinion differs from yours, so hush."

Tandi huffed. "Well, that settles it, then. You are an idiot and you're blind. Remind me why we're friends again because I don't do stupid very well."

Before I could get in an elementary argument with Tandi, I saw a shadow fall over our table. We both looked up slowly to see Jamison standing there with his arms crossed and a huge grin on his face. The expression on Tandi's face was triumphant. Mine was disbelieving.

His deep voice rumbled. "Listen, ladies, if both of you are going to talk about me where I can hear it, do you mind if I just join you for lunch?"

I felt my eyebrows scrunch together. There was no way he could have heard us.

As I sat there baffled, Tandi answered for us both. "Well, it wouldn't be very Southern of us if we said no, now would it? Pull you up a chair, hon. And I'm Tandi, by the way."

"I'm Jamison. It's a pleasure to meet you, Tandi," he said as he shook her hand, then he started sliding in the booth on my side. So much for pulling up a chair like Talon had done and Tandi had suggested.

I could refuse to move and make things awkward, or I could just scoot over. Manners won. "Oh. Okay. Here, let me just move over and make some room for you."

About that time, Jenny sauntered over to the table and set a hot plate in front of Jamison. She placed her palms on our table, leaning so close to him I thought for a second she was going to kiss him.

"Do you need anything else, big guy?" Jenny all but purred.

"Jenny, he doesn't need mouth-to-mouth. As you can see, the man is still breathing. Why don't you give him some space, unless you're trying to see if he can guess what you had for lunch?" Tandi asked.

Jenny glared at Tandi, and one side of Jamison's mouth twitched like he was trying his hardest not to laugh. When Jenny straightened away from him, he said, "Not right now, Jenny, thanks."

As Jenny turned to walk back to the kitchen, Tandi slapped her hand on the table. "Hold the phone. Where's our food? We were here way before he strolled in."

Jenny looked at Jamison like he was a piece of meat and when she finally peeled her eyes off of him, she muttered, "I figured waiting a little while wouldn't hurt you."

Tandi growled, "That's it, you good for nothing little—"

"I'm sure your food will be right out, Tandi," Jamison said. "Jenny probably didn't mean to slight you because that would be catty, and she seems like a real sweetheart."

Jenny stammered, "Y-yes. Yes, you're right. I'm very sweet. Tandi, Charlie, your food will be right out." And she scrambled away from the table.

Tandi unwrapped her silverware from her napkin, pointing a fork at Jamison. "I really hate her. I mean, there is like no love for her. I should have thrown my butter knife at her."

I gave Jamison a serious look. "When she's really fired up, she likes to throw things. It's best not to rile her any further to avoid possible injuries and to be able to leave this establishment in one piece."

Jamison let out a big belly laugh, causing Tandi to give him her legendary stank eye.

In her scary voice, she asked, "What? You don't think we're capable of unleashing terror?"

He put his hands up in defense. "No, I know you mean what you say. It's just funny. Here's two well-put together, beautiful ladies sitting in a family diner, speaking with major southern drawls, and to hear you say you're going to unleash terror on someone—even if the would-be victim is a catty waitress—well, that's just funny."

Tandi said, "Yeah, well, if you do have connections with a higher organization, now is as good a time as any to make a suggestion on who you should take out." At my frown, she said, "Hey, Jenny's had it coming for a long time. You know, before you…"Taking one finger out, she made a slicing motion across her throat. "…you should put a whole bunch of fish heads in the bed with her while she's sleeping to really convey a message."

"Oh, lord in heaven." I put a hand over my face and was surprised to hear Jamison chuckling. Giving him what I knew must have been a guilty look, I said, "I heard demolished, and my imagination went rampant. I'm sorry."

He shoveled in another bite of eggs. "It's fine. Don't worry about it. Imagination is great for the soul. I used to pretend that I was Sir Lancelot when I was little."

We all laughed at that until our food arrived, and then we started eating. When Jamison wasn't staring at me, which was ninety percent of the time, his eyes would roam the diner like he was looking for someone. I could tell by the weird look on Tandi's face she was about five seconds away from giving Jamison the third degree and was just thinking of a way to ease into her interrogation. I could see the train wreck coming; I just didn't know how to stop it, or if I really wanted to.

Finally, in between bites, she said, "So, Jamison, who is it that you keep looking for? A girlfriend?"

Unfortunately, I was taking a sip of sweet tea and started coughing on her last question. Jamison took me by surprise when he started patting me on the back. His touch was warm but other than that, nothing remotely interesting happened. I was starting to wonder if I'd imagined the jolt he gave me earlier. I waited for the tingling sensation but it never came.

"I thought there was someone here that I knew, but he must've already left." Jamison took up more than his fair share of the booth seat. His leg was practically touching mine when he stretched out.

I had stopped coughing, but he was still rubbing small circles on my back, so I twitched in my seat until he dropped his hand. His proximity flustered me. Not just because he was the most handsome boy I've ever seen but because his touch was almost comfortable. Like he knew me. I had been feeling so alone and depressed here recently that a comforting touch from a perfect stranger was more than startling.

Tandi slapped the table. "Well, color me intrigued."

"Dang!" I looked at my watch. "I've got to get to work."

Jamison pushed his plate away from him. "Where do you work?"

I sized him up, silently rating his stalker potential in my head. The town was small, so technically if he wanted to find out where I worked, he would have no problem getting the information.

I wadded up my napkin and put it on my plate, along with my dirty utensils. "I work at a shop on Main Street called Broom Sticks. They sell mostly natural herbs for anything that might ail you or help you in a natural, organic sort of way. Along with some knick-knacks. My brother hooked me up with the job, and so far I love it."

"Well, maybe we can talk at a better time. Thank you, ladies, for having dinner with me," he said as he signaled Jenny for the check. "I'm sure that I will see the both of you around."

"What are you doing here, if you don't mind me asking?" I blurted out.

His mouth opened and closed before his eyes searched my face—for what, I didn't know. Several seconds go by before he said, "I work with my family, and we're looking for an antique piece that is extremely valuable. We think it might have turned up in this town."

Tandi said, "If you don't know where to start, Charlie could help you. She's great at finding things."

My mouth dropped open. What in the world was wrong with Tandi? I somehow knew where that missing kid was, and now she thought I could find anything. She had called me twice this week looking for her car keys. And why would I help this boy? He might find out about my flaw. I thought about the card in my pocket. Maybe I should call Talon and request more information before Tandi started outing me to everybody.

Tandi leaned forward in her seat. Subtlety clearly not being her strong suit. "It wouldn't hurt to help look."

Jamison cleared his throat, breaking me from my thoughts. "I actually could use the help. Even if it was just as a tour guide."

"This town is so small you don't need anyone to show you around, and I'm not sure if I'm adequate for the job. Perhaps someone else would be better suited—"

"Yes, but I assume you probably know everyone and could open up some doors for me. I'll pay you a hundred dollars for every day you help me find what I'm looking for."

Tandi squealed. "Heck, yeah! When does she start?"

Still in a daze, I found myself utterly speechless. Why would this man pay me that much money when he isn't even sure that I can help him?

Jamison smiled at Tandi, and she winked in return. Let the conspiracy begin.

"How about right after you close? I can meet you at work," he said.

I glanced at Tandi, who was nodding her head so fast she looked like a bobble-head doll. "Well... I guess. We close at eight."

"Brooms Sticks on Main Street at eight." Jamison stood up from the booth. "I'm going to go find Jenny and take care of the bill. It's the least I could do for both of you allowing me to eat with you."

I was about to tell him no, that I could pay my own way, but yet again, Tandi beat me to the punch. "You're right. You couldn't have found better companionship in this whole measly place, so we won't argue with you, but I do ask that you don't tip that flat-faced, high-forehead, bucktooth Jenny too much."

He chuckled as I slid out of the booth, muttering a quick goodbye to the both of them. I headed to work, thinking about how crazy today was. Talon's offer couldn't have come at a better time if he'd planned it. Then again, maybe he did plan it. His offer was a little too good to be true. The more I thought about it, the more conflicted I felt. It would be so nice to wake up surrounded by people like me. I wouldn't have to hide who I'd become. I would feel connected... speaking of connections, I did feel a crazy one to Jamison, or maybe it was just my overactive teenage hormones. Either way, maybe I could help him find what it was he was looking for then decide if I should take Talon up on his offer.

chapter four

I was dusting off the glass cabinets that held some of my favorite trinkets. The whole store was neat, but the little golden elephants were my favorite. Elephants were so loyal and family oriented. Ever since I had lost my parents, I'd needed something. Craved it. I thought back to Talon and his offer; maybe they could be my herd. I heard the cowbell ring over the door of my shop. I looked up, and Brandon, my ex, walked through the door with a bouquet of red roses. His dark brown hair was perfectly styled, even during the harsh rainstorm we were currently suffering through. With his big brown eyes and perfectly asymmetrical face, he looked like the perfect, charismatic quarterback of Peu Springs who everyone seemed to love.

Just four hours earlier, I would have said he was the hottest thing in our small town, but that was before Talon showed up and definitely before Jamison.

Brandon handed me the bouquet of flowers. "Hey, pretty girl. I wanted to come by to see if you wanted to go to that fancy restaurant with me tonight after you close shop? I know it's your favorite."

I had told him a million times that we weren't a couple anymore, but he refused to really believe someone could actually dump him.

"Brandon, we're over, and I try not to make a habit of going out with ex-boyfriends."

He took a step forward and wrapped his hands around my back while I crossed my arms over my chest, ensuring there was at least some space between us.

"Please, let go of me."

"No. You're my girlfriend, and I can hold you if I want to. There are a lot of girls in this town that would be honored to be in your position. Maybe you need to remember that."

Something in me snapped. Ever since I broke up with him, he had been showing up everywhere he knew I would be. His head tilted towards mine, and I knew I was going to have to dodge another sloppy kiss yet again. He was becoming more and more aggressive since the breakup. Enough was enough. I put a hand on his face, trying to shove him away. I wanted him to leave me alone! I was shocked when I realized I had screamed this to the top of my lungs after a string of curse words.

He stopped right before his lips touched mine. His eyes glazed over, and then confusion wove over his face. He jumped back from me. "Who the hell are you?"

"Are you serious?"

His eyes held a bewildered look. "I don't know you. Why was I holding you? Did you do something to me?"

My hand covered my mouth. Did I do something to him? I really wanted him to forget about me and move on, and now he was looking at me as if I had two heads.

He gave me a disgusted look before storming out of the shop. I slid down to the floor, my back resting against the counter. I was out of control. I wasn't upset that I clearly just did something to Brandon. In my mind, he had it coming. He should feel thankful that I didn't set him on fire like I did the family album. I'm upset that I had zero control. What if I accidentally harmed someone that I loved? I would call Talon and tell him I'd take him up on his offer. I didn't care at this point what the training entailed. Tears trailed down my face. I wish my parents were here. I wish they could help me figure out what was wrong with me.

That's how Jamison found me hours later. When the cowbell rang again, I almost banged my head on the counter.

"I'm sorry I frightened you." Jamison put both of his hands in his jean pockets, as if to put me at ease. If he noticed I'd been crying, he didn't say anything. He nodded towards the roses now scattered across the floor. "You don't strike me as a rose kind of girl."

I stood up on shaky legs. "Well, Jamison, who I don't even know your last name, what kind of flower do you think I like?"

"Daisies." His forehead crinkled as his eyes roamed over my body like he was checking for damage. I wanted to say I wasn't hurt on the outside, but there was something very wrong on the inside. His nose was flaring as he took deep breaths. "And it's Bradford."

"What's Bradford?"

He smiled. "My last name."

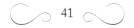

He came to stand right before me. "You want to talk about what just happened?"

Did I? I chose to remain silent. How could I go wrong with that option?

He sighed before he changed the subject. "You ready to help me find what I'm looking for?" He pulled out an envelope, placing it on the counter. "That's the first week's payment."

I frowned. "A hundred dollars a day? That just sounds crazy. Besides, how do you even know that I can help you find what you're looking for?"

"Let's just say that I have a good feeling about you."

I crossed my arms over my chest as my toe tapped the floor.

"Okay, okay. How about because I know that you might not be exactly what you seem, and that's because I'm not exactly what I seem, either. And as far as the money, well, you're worth it. Even if you don't contribute anything to finding the lost object, at least I'll be in your company."

I had stopped listening after he said that I might not be "exactly what I seem." What was going on? Was I a freaking beacon? A homing device? Did everyone all of a sudden know that I was different? I grabbed hold of the counter to steady myself.

"Whoa, are you okay? Talk to me. What's going on?"

"I... I don't know anything anymore. I think you need to leave."

"Charlie, I think you do know what I'm talking about, and I also think you're in need of a friend right now, so I can either wait here with you while you call your friend Tandi, or you can give me a shot."

When I didn't say anything, he walked to the door, flipped the sign to closed, and turned the lock. I should have been freaked out by his authoritative demeanor, but I was too busy wigging out over the fact that men in hazmat suits might show up at my door to cart me off to a lab. I was over here frying bigger fish.

He stayed on the other side of the room, perhaps to look less threatening, if that was even possible for him. "I know I'm right about you, but aren't you even a little curious to see how I know I'm right?"

"Another boy showed up today. His name is Talon. Are you friends? Or part of the same marketing team? Scouts for freaks?"

His blue eyes met mine. His jaws clenched and for a moment, I didn't think he would answer me. Finally, he released a breath. "Talon was here? They work fast."

"Who's they?"

He shook his head. "Is there somewhere we could sit and talk?"

What could it hurt? "I have a little break room in the back."

"Lead the way, love, and if you don't like what I'm saying at any time, I'll leave. All right?"

Catching the hopeful look in his eyes, I nodded. "Come on back, and I'll make you a cup of coffee while we talk."

He followed me back to my little quiet place, which was all pink floral walls, white cottage furniture, and a matching couch.

He started tugging on his snug, black T-shirt. "Are you going to confiscate my balls at the door?"

I laughed. "This room is a tad girly." At his eye roll, I said, "Okay, it's probably the most girly room in America, but with a name like Charlie, it's pushed all my girly instincts into overdrive. The owner of this place told me to decorate the break room anyway I like, so I did."

He stared at the pink walls as if they were closing in on him. "I think I can manage in this room for short periods of time. I'll just focus on what you're saying, and I won't let my eyes roam off of you for any reason."

I stopped pouring his coffee and looked over my shoulder.

Jamison threw his hands up. "Hey, my extreme attention to you is just to help me keep my manhood."

I seriously doubted this man had any problem with his manhood, but I refused to go down that road. I needed to focus. I handed him his coffee and sat on the opposite end of the couch. So many questions ran through my head, but as I looked at him, I hesitated. Where to begin?

"You found me in a weird state of mind. It's been a rough day."

"I couldn't smell any blood, so I knew that you weren't hurt. I figured if you wanted to tell me, you would."

"An ex-boyfriend is having a hard time being an ex."

His eyes turned to steel. "Do you need me to handle it?"

"No." That was part of the problem. I think I handled it. Wait. Did he say smell?

"It's not hard reading your facial expressions. You would be a horrible poker player." He gave me a smile riddled with encouragement. "What is it you want to know?"

After clearing my throat, I asked, "How could you smell if I was hurt? I might not be a poker player, but I'm going to ask you to lay out your cards first. You need to know that I hate lies. Tell me exactly what… what you are."

He took his first sip of coffee, studying me over the rim. He leaned back against the couch cushions, grinning at my apparent discomfort. "What do you think I am?"

"Something… different." I shrugged my shoulders, trying to act like all of this was completely normal. "I don't know. A psychic?"

"Nope." He started laughing and my face flamed. "Sorry. That's hilarious."

Great, he was laughing at me. He probably thought I was crazy. Maybe I was insane. Ever since I turned eighteen, I knew there was a good chance I would end up in an insane asylum. I was still debating my sanity when he said, "I'm a werewolf."

The hell you say. "I'm sorry; what was that?"

Forget me being crazy—this lunatic in front of me was the real deal. I started gauging the distance between me and the door. If I was fast, I could possibly be out the door and halfway through the shop before he began to chase me.

"I'm a fast runner, love. Now, that we've started this conversation, I aim to finish it."

And he said he wasn't a psychic!

"Sure." I gulped. Maybe I could entertain him enough with this crazy conversation until the opportunity came to escape. Trying to fake calmness, I asked, "So, when you say werewolf, do you mean turning into a wolf during the full moon and howling, or what?"

"I'm one of the two most powerful werewolves in the world. I have been genetically altered, so my full wolf form is not like other werewolves, or what has been portrayed on the movie screens. Think more Hulk and less hair. My brother's body and mine enlarge along with our canines. We have an abundance of strength, speed, and are immortal. Our senses... well, they're all extremely heightened. For example, I can sense your fear right now, but I swear to you that you have nothing to be afraid of."

I swallowed a lump forming in my throat. "I guess I'll have to take your word on that. So, you're suggesting that the world has werewolves?"

"Not suggesting, love. I'm telling you there are werewolves—packs of them, and you have a live one right in front of you." He raked a hand through his shaggy hair. "Would you like to know what you are?"

Did I? Here was the moment I'd been waiting for, and yet I found myself panicking. There would be no turning back after this conversation. Stalling the only way I knew how, I asked, "How old are you exactly? Nineteen? Twenty?"

"Are you going to freak out if I tell you I'm one thousand, six hundred and eighty-four?"

Freak out? I was still digesting the werewolf thing. "Maybe."

"Okay, then. I'm twenty."

"My brain is having a hard time processing all of this."

"Maybe if I showed you what I am, it would help?" At my nod, his blue eyes turned a rich copper color, and his body seemed to grow. I watched in shock as his wide shoulders became even larger. Then in an instant, like a balloon that had been popped, his eyes were back to blue, and there was a grin on his face. "I can demonstrate more if you would like?"

I could feel myself starting to panic; he scooted over on the couch and laid a hand on my shoulder. A calmness overcame me. My eyes jerked to his. "Are you doing this?"

"Yes. Another talent of mine."

"A walking bottle of Valium."

"Do you mind? I can stop."

"No, keep the happy juice flowing." I took a couple of deep breaths. "All right, so you're a genetically altered werewolf." Not going to lie. Didn't see that coming. "What am I?"

I made a mental promise to myself that whatever his next few words were, I wouldn't freak out. I hated making promises I couldn't keep.

chapter five

"Y ou are a witch."

Ha! That was funny. A witch? Like, burn me at the stake witch? Or like warts on my nose witch? I tuned back into what he was saying.

"The witch family host many different breeds. The psychic you accused me of being falls under the witch category, along with mind readers and telekinetics. Only the strongest of the witches are presumed to have some sort of royalty in them. Your powers are extreme. There is no doubt when your body is fully done transitioning, you will be a powerful witch."

"Why would you think I'm a witch?"

"Well, you don't look like a demon, and your ears aren't pointed like the fae. Plus, you have the smell of witchery, and I can tell by the energy leaking out of your pores." At my look, he said, "Maybe that was too much at once."

"Yeah, maybe. It's like there is a whole new world of beings out there. I thought I was just born with an extra sense, or maybe a gene was mutated, but what you're suggesting makes me sound like I am a part of a whole different race." This was crazy. Ludicrous. I felt like I was losing some of my sanity by just thinking what he said could be true.

Taking another sip of his coffee, he studied me. "Being a witch is hereditary, like so many other unworldly beings. Meaning that one of your parents would have to be a witch."

"Well, both of my parents are dead, so there's no way I can fact check that tidbit of info you just gave me." Rubbing my forehead, I asked, "What else you got?"

His lips raised in an amused smile. "Being a witch can't be too far of a stretch of your imagination, can it? If you think back all the way from childhood, I'm sure you can come up with numerous incidents that just didn't add up."

Well, I would give him that. "There were a few times when I noticed something different in me. Sometimes, things would happen that a… normal person shouldn't have been able to do. But since I turned eighteen, things have gone from weird to scary."

His voice was quiet, as if I was a rabbit he didn't want to scare away. "Like what things?"

"When I was little, my brother noticed I had a crazy intuition. I've also never been sick. But then after I turned eighteen, I've been able to create things. Like fog, ice, and fire." Just saying it out loud to someone other than Tandi made me want to vomit. "I thought it was something to do with the temperature in my body being abnormal."

"Is there anything else?" he asked.

Was he serious? That was quite a lot of eccentric abilities I just listed and if anyone else were sitting there, they would have called the psych ward and had me locked up.

I inwardly groaned. "Maybe. I found a lost kid once. But I haven't really 'found' anything since then. Then tonight, something new happened." I explained to him about Brandon. His nose flaring a couple of times was the only sign of emotion he gave.

He placed his mug on my glass coffee table. "How many people have seen or know of your powers?"

That word "power" was still giving me a hard time. "Tandi—she knows that there's… something different about me." We'd been friends since kindergarten, and despite the way Tandi flounced around, she was a borderline genius. It didn't take her long to start giving me the calculating look she doles out.

I didn't mention the fact Tandi was convinced I had some kind of superhero powers currently dormant and when they awoke, she was going to open up her own circus ring and make me the main attraction. She swore we could travel the world and make money, and me being me, I hated to burst her bubble, so I just went with it. She was going to be so disappointed when she learned that there was a cap to my abilities and I couldn't sprout wings and fly or shoot fire from my mouth. Who was I kidding? Knowing Tandi, she would still find a way to capitalize off of my freakish abilities.

"Then Talon approached me earlier today and now you."

Suspicion colored his voice. "Let me guess; he is here to offer you a spot in his training camp?"

"Yes."

He mumbled something under his breath about another pawn. "You claimed to have a strong intuition. What do you think of Talon?"

I thought back to the young, handsome boy. "He knows what he wants and how to get it. There is a darkness in him, but I'm not sure how deep it goes." To be fair, there was darkness in all of us. "He gave me an ultimatum earlier. He said I needed to make a decision quick, and then the offer would be off the table. That was a lie."

"Charlie, tell me this; what's your gut saying to you right now? About me?"

There was no need to think about my answer. "It's telling me you've been speaking the truth, but you're full of secrets."

"Then know that I speak the truth when I say you would be making a horrible mistake to trust Talon. He will only lead you down a path of destruction."

My gut was saying that I could trust him. But my gut didn't say not to trust Talon. Ugh.

One thing at a time. "Let's back up to the demon part. You're saying these actually exist, also? As in red people with black horns?"

One massive shoulder hiked up. "Maybe the baby demons, but the older ones… the ones that are centuries old; they can take on any form." A frown marred his striking features. "Those are the dangerous ones because they could be a baseball coach, a preacher, or your neighbor."

I glanced down at my faded blue jeans and cowgirl boots. Maybe I wasn't ready for this world. But I knew there was no chance I could leave this room as the same girl who'd entered. I took a shaky breath. "I always just assumed that there was something wrong with me. I've spent the last couple months of my life trying to act normal, afraid I was two steps away from the looney bin. It was impossible to talk to my brother."

Jamison's eyebrows shot up. "And why is that, Charlie?"

"We've been through a lot since our parents died. He has taken on a ton of responsibilities, including being my guardian. I couldn't talk to him about this."

"You do realize there is a good chance your brother is a witch. The only way he could escape that fate is if one of your parents was human, some other kind of supernatural, or he was adopted. Or maybe you were adopted?"

No. I looked like my mother, and my brother looked exactly like my father. My brother couldn't be a witch. He would have told me. There was no way.

Rubbing my sweaty palms down my jeans, I stood up from the couch, putting some distance between us. The second I didn't feel his touch anymore, all calmness left my body, and nervous energy replaced it. I sat on top of my desk, facing Jamison.

"When I first touched you, it was like you electrocuted me. A jolt ran up my arm. Did you feel it?"

He shook his head. "Can't say that I did."

"Hmm. I told you I hated lies."

His eyebrows rose, but he didn't dispute his last comment. After everything he had told me, why would he lie about something like this? I tilted my head, studying him. There was something pretentious about his relaxed pose on the couch. He was so tightly coiled, as if he was ready to pounce. He came off as primitive and wild. A being that could never be tamed, and his last sentence sat false in my stomach. But again, why would he lie?

"Is there anything else you can tell me about witches?"

I tried not to notice how he relaxed as I changed the subject. "Most witches are not immortal, but they live hundreds of years." Shrugging his massive shoulders, he added, "Also, most witches live in communities together. That's when they are the strongest. Your parents, for whatever reason, decided to move away from their community to here, where they were more vulnerable. It's strange."

What he wasn't saying left me feeling sick to my stomach. Was it possible that my parents weren't killed in a random act of violence? I was taking too much information in at one time, and this was something I was going to have to shelve and come back to at a later date. If I thought of their death right now, I would be done for the rest of the day. Those memories sent me spiraling down into a world of depression that was too hard to fight my way through. It was like a tidal wave crashing against the rocks and if I wasn't careful, my memories would drown me.

As if he could sense my turmoil, his lips turned down in a frown. "What is it that your brother does?"

"Wes is an artist. He used to be a struggling one until here recently. He got noticed by some big-wig up North and is now selling his paintings in an art gallery." He was always traveling, and I missed the big lug.

He ran a hand down his face, releasing a loud sigh. "I don't want to freak you out more than you already are, but I need you to know that you're probably not safe here. Especially if Talon has already sought you out."

"What are you suggesting?"

"I'm just giving you options. You don't have to take Talon up on his offer. Gather all the information you can, then make your decision. I would like to put an offer on the table as well. I could train you. Teach you about the supernatural community."

Oh, but my gut told me he had an ulterior motive. "Yeah, and what do you get out of it?"

"Besides your time?" His expression makes me blush. His eyes seem to be scorching my skin. "You will help me locate that object I was telling you about."

My eyes narrowed. He was speaking the truth, but I wasn't getting all of it. "If I decide that I don't want this… can you take my powers away from me?"

"No. And why would you want that? But I can teach you how to control them."

I was confused. "But Talon said that he could take away my powers if should decide to go that route."

His attitude changed instantly and his voice became almost stern. "The only way someone could release you of your powers is if they were a power eliminator which I assure you he is not or if they killed you. Do not ever trust Talon."

I hold his gaze for several moments before nodding. My gut said to trust Jamison.

Hopping off the desk, I went to grab his empty cup from him but instead found my hand entrapped by his warm one. Jamison gave my hand a gentle squeeze before asking, "So, are you willing to use your powers again to help me find what I'm looking for?"

Staring at our clasped hands, I thought of everything he had just told me. There was a good chance that I could learn how to control these powers, and there was an even better chance that if I didn't figure out how to use my powers soon, I could hurt someone.

I looked into his blue eyes, and I answered with my gut. "Yes." In a lighter tone, I said, "I help you and you help me."

"Yes, a give and take." There was amusement in his voice. Were we still talking about the same thing? His sexy smirk implied not. Oh, boy. He gently pulled me down onto the couch beside him. My palms began to sweat at his proximity. "What I'm seeking is very dangerous, but I can make a promise to you that as long as you stick close by me, no harm will come to you."

"Got it. Close to you." Did that come out squeaky?

His lips turned up into a smile as he gripped my hand and leaned forward. I sit frozen in place as he tucks my hair behind my ear. "Yep. Super close. We will be like glue before it's all said and done." The thrill his words create in me have me panicking and I find myself comically launching back from him. He gives me a wolfish smile letting me know that this boy whole-heartedly understands the impact he has on the fairer sex.

I needed space. After I disentangled my hand I cleared my throat. "Give me some background info on what I'll be looking for."

"Not tonight. You're about to overload as it is. Tomorrow, we will start with your training and searching for the object I need. But since I have nowhere that I would rather be, we can get to know one another on a more personal level." His eyebrows wiggle causing me to laugh.

"Sorry, that's not going to happen." I was proud of myself. My voice came out steady and I was showing self-control around the hottest male I've ever seen. I should win a prize. Maybe the Nobel one.

He stood up to his full height which put me eye level with his stomach and stretched. Like a creeper I watched him. Just because I had restraint didn't mean I was blind. I wanted to demand that we finish this conversation. I wanted to know what I was getting into before it was too late to back out, but the words died on my tongue as his shirt rode up, showing a perfect, flat belly with chiseled muscles. How did one even know which exercises to perform to get those kinds of muscles? No one should be that beautiful; it just wasn't right.

Before he headed out the door, he said, "Oh, and Charlie, one more thing. You better hope that your persuasion over Brandon holds because if it doesn't, I'll handle him." My stomach clenched with worry and something else that made me feel confused and excited at the same time. "See you tomorrow night."

chapter six

The next morning, I lay in bed way after my alarm clock went off, having a "how the hell did I end up here?" moment. I got good grades in school, flossed my teeth once a day, and said my prayers every night before I went to sleep. Now, I'd verbally agreed to work with a werewolf—a freaking real-life werewolf—to find a secret object. My mind had gone rampant last night thinking of what Jamison could possibly be after. I seriously doubted it was an antique lamp. With the way my luck had been going, I wouldn't be surprised if it was Pandora's box. I could hear the kids at school now, "Hey Charlie what's up? What did you do over the holiday break?" Then I would have to answer, "oh, nothing much. Just unleashing hell to poor innocents." Yeah, no. I should have found out what he was searching for before agreeing to help him.

I finally climbed out of bed as my cell phone pinged yet again. I grabbed it off the nightstand to see that Talon had not only figured out a way to get my cell, but he had texted me more than fifteen messages. Well, that's not creepy or anything. Maybe I should be totally excited someone was trying to recruit me so hard, considering that no sports scouts in their right mind would ever give me any attention. On the athletic scale, I was somewhere in the negative range. However, his tenacity didn't make me feel like Serena Williams, it made me want to close the blinds. I decided not to respond. Maybe he would take the hint and chill.

Thirty minutes later, I had showered, dressed, and was pulling into my school. The student parking section was tiny, so all the good spots were already taken. I parked my family-sized sedan next to the dumpster and made a run for class. I really couldn't afford to be late twice in a row.

I was a tad shocked to see Talon had somehow managed to enroll in my classes, as in every single one of them. He also finagled his way to my lunch table. It was when he set his tray down on the table and took a seat next to me that my inner voice warned me that this had all the makings for a creepy Lifetime movie. "Is this seat taken?"

I ignored his question hoping he would take the hint. He must get a huge commission for every trainee he brought back to the camp because he was straight-up hardcore when it came to getting my attention. If he was trying to win me over this was the wrong way to do it. My nerves were beginning to fray.

Tandi raked her carrots onto my plate before she snatched one of my cookies. That was so not an equal trade, but she could tell Talon was starting to annoy me. I guessed she saw a moment of distraction and went for it. I made a mental note to get her back.

Finally, Tandi broke the silence. "What's up, face?" Tandi said, as she ate the last of my chocolate chip chewy. "You coming to promote your facility—again?"

Jamison was mouth-watering hot. Ruggedly handsome. But Talon almost looked like a Ken doll. Pretty, but… fake? Plus, he made my radar go off. Everything about him from his wide smile to his mannerisms was a red flag. I was so comfortable with Jamison. When I talked with him it was like talking with an old friend. But Talon? No, I didn't trust him.

"Ladies, I'm not being too aggressive, am I?"

Tandi was never one to mince words. "Seriously, I think you passed 'a little' aggressive awhile back."

Talon looked to me for confirmation. "It's true. Switching to all of my classes is a little more than just tenacious."

He tried to disarm us with a smile. "I'm truly sorry if I am being too forward, but time is ticking, and I just want to make sure that if Charlie does turn our training camp down, I can at least say I did my very best in trying to get her to join us."

"What's the huge rush?"

"Our new session is soon to start and I just don't want you to miss out on this wonderful opportunity."

I started to tell him that I had found someone less pushy to train me, but I somehow managed to keep my mouth shut. "How about this? Give me a day just to think about what you have said. I really don't want to talk about it anymore right now. Does that sound fair?"

His eyebrows rose in concentration, and I almost told him to cool his jets, but he saved me from embarrassing us both. "Yeah, that's fair. I think I'll skip out on the rest of the day. I really was dreading geometry. At my old high school, I barely sat through that class the first time."

We all laughed, and it broke the tension. He finished eating with us, and then he parted ways. Tandi watched him as he exited the cafeteria. "Too bad he's not mute."

I laughed before I could catch myself then I grew serious. "Don't for one second think I'm going to let you get away with eating my cookie. Somehow, you'll pay for that, friend."

"Diabetes is a problem that I was trying to help you avoid. That's what good friends do. They take the bullet for one another. In this case, it was a cookie."

I bit the inside of my mouth to keep me from grinning. "Yeah, whatever."

She stood up with her tray in hand. "Oh, and it was plural. There were two cookies. I only got caught snatching one."

That heifer. Some things just crossed a line, friend or not. I was smiling as the remainder of my day flew by without Talon breathing down my neck or giving me that blank stare I caught him doing so often. More than once I caught myself thinking of a different boy. One that looked like a sinful angel who made my heart race.

I daydreamed about that angel all the way through my shift at work. Five minutes before closing, he showed up. He wore faded jeans and another soft cotton shirt. This time the fabric was white. I realized that I was staring and turned, so he couldn't see my blush.

"Just let me finish clocking out, and then we can sit and talk for a second. I'd like to know about this object you're looking for."

"Take your time, I'm in no rush." He strolled through the shop, looking at all the little trinkets. I had a hard time taking my eyes off of him, but I made myself go through closing. Finally when I was finished, I made a motion for him to take a seat in one of the two huge chairs by the cash register. I took the opposite one, facing him.

"You don't want to go out to eat? Or somewhere more comfortable?" he asked.

I was too nervous to eat, and I was scared I would throw myself at him if we were going for comfort. "Nope. I'm good. I have been anxious all day, waiting to hear what you're looking for."

He reached out and grabbed the leg of my chair, scooting me closer to him. Then he held onto one of my hands. Lust hit me full throttle. If my heartbeat got any faster, I would pass out and wouldn't that be embarrassing. "I'm looking for a very important key." His sigh was heavy, as if he didn't know where to begin. "This has to remain between me, you, and I guess Tandi, considering that you've probably never kept anything from her. If you trust her, then so do I."

With a sheepish smile, I said, "Not going to lie, I can't keep anything from her, but I can promise you I would never blab my mouth about you or what you're after, and I know Tandi wouldn't either."

"I believe you." He stretched out his long jean-clad legs on either side of my chair. "I guess I need to explain some things. Get you up to speed. Right now, there's a war between the factions that's imminent. Small wars have already taken place between the Degenerates and the Lux. If you had grown up in a witch community, you would have learned about all of this. The Degenerates are evil creatures, like demons, ghouls, rogue vampires, and even though my brother is reigning King of the Werewolves, some of the wolves have turned to the Degenerates' side. The Lux are mostly made up of fae, shapeshifters, and vampires. Like I said, the witch community covers many different supernaturals: healers, mind readers, telekinetics. Most witches are on the Lux side but, like everything in life, there are some bad apples."

It was hard for me to take it all in, but I tried. "So, what exactly is everybody fighting for?"

He still refused to release my hand, and now he was making small circles with his thumb on the inside of my wrist, sending shivers through me. With one simple touch and I almost felt bare. How is that even possible? I should pull my hand away, but I didn't. His voice penetrated my thoughts. Focus, Charlie. Focus! "The Degenerates have a hard time not destroying everything they come into contact with. As a whole, they've decided to take over the world. They began by attacking the leaders of all the different Lux factions. The Degenerates think if they can kill the Lux leaders, as well as collect all the keys, then they can overpower what's left of each faction to create, basically, one Degenerate army. We can't let that happen. Not only will the Lux be hunted down and killed, but no human will be safe."

"What's so important about these keys? What exactly do they open? And why do you think Peu Springs has your key?"

"There are seven keys total the Lux have to track down. Technically, there are six now, since my brother, CG, has the first one in his possession. All the keys used to have guardians, but the Degenerates slowly started killing the keepers, one by one, to claim the keys for themselves. There are forty-nine portals all over the world, and the keys can open up any of those portals to different planes. Here's the problem: some of the vilest supernaturals are on those planes. They were banished there by the strongest Lux. Think of it as a human prison. When a supernatural commits a crime that breaks the rules of the supernatural realm, they have to go to one of the forty-nine portals. Lesser evils go to the lower-numbered portals. The higher numbered the portal the worse the plane is because that's where the evilest beings reside. If the Degenerates hold the keys, they can open up the portals and free their friends—the felons who were once banished from earth. Then they have the freedom to come here and wreak havoc, mostly on humans. In the last year, there have been a lot of John and Jane Does turning up in morgues everywhere. I fear that there might be even more in the future."

If he feared something then I should be terrified. I shook my head. "Let me get this straight. You're saying the Lux have to find a total of seven keys or earth will be like a huge frat house, but with murder and mayhem?"

"Yeah, that's one way of putting it."

I blew a stray piece of hair out of my face. "Well, no offense, but it seems like the Lux didn't do too good of a job protecting the keys in the first place. What makes you think that they will do a better job of it this go around?"

"The last go around, the Lux trusted the wrong people. I think we've learned our lesson. Plus, Ariana—she's like my and my brother's grandmother—she's been looking out for us since we were little. She's a soothsayer. She can see all and is in charge of picking who will control the keys this time. Like a gamekeeper, she picks and chooses who can be entrusted with the keys."

I felt sweat trickle down my back. Sitting this close to him was like being placed in a furnace. My forehead wrinkled. "You still didn't answer me. Why do you think one of the keys is located here in Peu Springs?"

"Sorry, Ariana can not only see the future clearly, but she can also control what she sees. She told me that I needed to go to South America, so I packed a duffel bag and immediately headed out."

"What was in South America?" I asked.

"A man who knew where a key was located. But that's not the reason she sent me. The man was trafficking small children, and Ariana has a soft spot for all children. She could have just told me the real reason why she wanted me to go, but sometimes, I feel like she is so used to manipulating us to do what she wants she forgets how to just ask."

"Who in this town could possibly have the key?"

"That's what I'm hoping you will help me find out."

"So, this man in South America just gave you some serious, heavy-duty information and then what?"

"I demolished some things," he said. "And before you ask what happened to the man, ask only if you really want to know."

It was like knowing most gummy bears had a certain percentage of bugs in them. Once you knew that, you couldn't un-know it, and now I couldn't enjoy the candy without gagging a little. So, no. I didn't want to know. "All right, so we find the key and we're done?"

"Yes, but I promise you it won't be that easy."

"How do we start?"

"Why don't you start by telling me how you found the missing kid?"

"It was actually Tandi who suggested that I try. When something is missing, I concentrate on the object and can somehow hone in on it. But anything that I've ever found has been mine, or I have been close to it, like the child. I felt a strong connection to him since I sometimes babysat him and his older sister. I'm not sure how it would work with something I've never seen or have a connection to."

"It's worth a shot." He acted as if he wanted to say more, but instead he gave my hand a gentle squeeze. "I've given you a lot of information in a short amount of time. Would it be all right with you if I came to your house tomorrow around six, and we can get started?"

I felt a little disappointed I wouldn't be spending more time with him, but I tried to mask it. "Sure."

Obviously, my face betrayed me. I glanced up at Jamison who was laughing while looking at me with such heat in his gaze. "Trust me I don't want to go, but if I stay I can't promise that I'll behave as a gentleman."

I was waiting for my cheeks to catch on fire when he placed a finger under my chin, tilting my face up slowly, forcing me to look into his eyes. His piercing gaze had me licking my lips, drawing his attention there before he abruptly stood up. He jammed his hands in his pockets as he cleared his throat.

The silence between us became long and drawn out. I had to say something. Anything to ease the tension. "So, training tomorrow?"

His blue eyes were swirling with honey. "Hmm? Oh, yeah. I've been thinking about the location of your training. I think it's best to start out in the country where no one will stumble upon us. Can you get out of work tomorrow? Then we could start your training and look for the key."

I bit my lip. I'd love to, but I really loved this job. Plus, the old lady who owned the store really relied on me and to call in with such short notice… I just couldn't.

"I have to work tomorrow, but we can meet at my house afterward. Then the next day, we can begin training."

So many emotions flittered over his face and I would have given anything to know exactly what he was thinking. "Promise me you won't do anything rash like joining Talon's group until you've given me a chance to work with you."

"What do you have against Talon?"

"That's a great question that deserves a lengthy answer. How about as an extra incentive, I'll answer some of your questions if you learn something new while I'm training you? That sounds fair to me."

It sounded more like stalling to me, but I let it slide. For now. "I guess that's what old people do, huh? They try to keep a little mystery in their lives, so us youngsters won't grow bored."

His bark of laughter had me smiling. "I'll show you old on training day."

Something in his blue eyes made my stomach clench. There was mischief there, along with some kind of unspoken promise. Man, he was hot. His nose flared briefly. Just in case he was that psychic he claimed he wasn't, I jumped up from my chair with a fake yawn.

"Whoa, look at the time."

He grinned as he stood. "Come on, and I'll walk you to your car."

After I had locked up the shop, he walked me down the street to where my car was parked. He held the door open for me and, right before he closed it, his full lips curled into a sly smile. "You are making it so hard to behave." He gave a humorless laugh while he raked a hand down his face. "You know I can smell pheromones, right?"

Thank goodness it was night-time because I'm sure my face was crimson. "Um, no I didn't know that. But thanks for that interesting detail. I don't know what I'll do with it, but I'll definitely file it away."

I slammed my car door, not caring if I got his fingers or not. I tried not to notice his smirk as I started my car and pulled out. Being a teenager was a hard life. But awkwardness got cranked up to an all-time high when you were crushing on someone, and they could literally smell it. I had a feeling this would be another long night without sleep. My embarrassment would see to it.

chapter seven

The next day at school, Talon waited for me after my first class. I thought I internalized my groan, but since he was scowling, I might've slipped up. He wore a polo shirt with jeans and looked as if he could fit in easily with Peu Springs' wealthiest.

"Have you given any thought about my offer?"

I shifted my books in my arms. "Yes, actually I have. I want to train. I want to learn who I am, and if at the end of the day, I still don't like who I am, your offer of eliminating my—" I glanced around the hall to the other kids. He smiled at me, and with a wave of his hand, he put us in a bubble like the one at the diner. "Thanks. Your offer of eliminating my powers sounds perfect, but let me ask you, how do you plan on doing that, exactly?"

His practiced smile annoyed me. "I have some connections. People that can help you."

My gut was saying that he was lying through his perfectly straight teeth. I clenched my fist in my lap. Just exactly what was his game? Why lie to me?

"Well honestly, I can't just pick up and leave my brother and Tandi."

He gave me a charming smile. "I'm not going to take no for an answer. I'm going to persuade you. Eventually, you will thank me." He took my books from me. "Come on. I'll walk you to class. Promise you will save me a seat at lunch?"

Having a hot boy carry your books was nothing to complain over but here I was again feeling aggravated. Maybe it was the lack of sleep I got last night. I'd tossed and turned half the night, replaying my conversation with Jamison. The bags under my eyes were from the revelations I learned, not from remembering how his touch seemed to leave me hot and confused at the same time, and how he seemed to know exactly what he was doing to me. I had boyfriends in the past, but this was the first time I had ever felt an attraction like this. Every time I was around him I was scared that I would burst into flames.

Oops. Talon was still waiting for my answer. "Yeah, sure. Sounds good."

He looked a little put out over my lack of enthusiasm, but I was in no mood to smooth his feathers. This day couldn't possibly go any slower.

My day went by at a snail's pace and so did work. I'd thought less about my powers and more about my soon-to-be trainer than I would like to admit, even to Tandi who was currently at my house.

"Listen, why do I have to be here when Mr. Boy Toy comes over?" Tandi whined.

I had made Tandi come over to my house after I got off of work. She had reluctantly helped me straighten up before flopping on my couch, swearing she wasn't built for domestic life, and she had to stop before she started sweating because she wasn't built for that, either.

Reaching down, I took her sandals off of her feet. All I needed was dirt on our white couch. Tandi always said, "The higher the hair, the closer to God," and my motto was more like "cleanliness is next to godliness." To each their own.

"For the umpteenth time, I don't want to be alone with him. He makes me a little nervous with all those smoldering gazes and innuendoes he throws my way. It's hard to concentrate with him around." Plus, having her in the room would kill those pheromones leaking from my body without my permission.

Tandi narrowed her eyes at me. "Um, thanks? So, I'm like your chastity belt."

I threw my hands up in the air. "What the hell are you talking about?"

"Whoa! Hello, angry? Mad much?" She waved an arm at me. "Simmer down. Now, tell me what it was Face was talking to you about today."

"You mean Talon?"

"Yeah, who else? Ironically, the angel has a better face than Face, but since I've already dubbed him that, I can't change it now. It would be just too confusing for everybody."

I wanted to ask her who everybody was, but I decided it wasn't worth it. "So Talon asked me if I was ready to leave with him, and I told him the truth. I'm conflicted. I don't want to leave my home."

"Honestly, though, would you have said yes if the angel hadn't propositioned you, too? Admit it. The angel had some sway on you staying here."

"He just gave me another option is all." I tried to sound all nonchalant, but I wasn't fooling her. "All I have to do is help him find this key, which really, I would help him with anyways, if what he said about it getting in the wrong hands is true."

"You need to step outside of your comfort zone. Get drunk off of a bottle with a worm in it. Send me home and put on something that shows a little leg."

I threw a couch pillow at her. "Just stop." I pointed a finger at her. "You know if what Jamison said is true and I am a powerful witch, once I learn how to uncloak these badass powers, I could abracadabra some facial hair on you."

"I think I could pull off facial hair. Me and my goatee would open up my traveling circus and become famous, and then I would have very little time on my hands to listen to all your woes."

"You are exhausting. Maybe I shouldn't have asked you to come."

Tandi threw her hands up. "Hello, darling, that is exactly what I've been preaching. You don't need me here. I am a mood killer. You need to light a couple of candles and put on some 'drop it like it's hot' music." I thought she saw my eye starting to twitch because she changed the subject. "Well, since we have an hour before he shows up, why don't you help me practice my lines?"

I walked to the kitchen and started pulling out ingredients for a cheese plate. That girl jumped subjects so fast, my head spun. "What lines?"

She huffed. "Remember, I'm taking theater this semester? Well, I tried out for the musical The Little Mermaid, and I got the part of Scuttle."

I stopped rolling the meat. "I'm sorry, what?"

She got up from the couch and sauntered in, putting her hands on her curvy hips. "I know. I so thought I was an Ariel. But whatever."

"Tandi, you can't sing."

She grabbed her chest. "Maybe I can, and you're just tone deaf."

"Um, no I'm pretty sure you can't sing. Like at all. That's probably why they cast you as the bird. I mean, even the crab has more lines, right?"

"Girl, we're about to have a come-to-Jesus meeting." She flipped her hair behind her. "If you're not going to help me with my lines, why don't you tell me what the plan is for you to find this key? You know who I would start interrogating?"

A pounding pain started behind my eyes, and I felt a headache coming on, but against my better judgment, I said, "Who?"

Tandi's eyebrows shot to her hairline. "The preacher's son. Who is also the assistant pastor."

"Donnie? He's like the sweetest guy ever. Why in the world would he have the key?"

"Because what better cover up than being a man of God? I mean, look at your face right now. You're registering total disbelief. And besides that, last month

I called him to ask if the Garden Club could have their bingo night in the Church's fellowship hall, and get this, he said no!"

Putting my own acting skills to bat, I feigned shock. "No way. You're telling me that Donnie didn't want gambling done in the church?"

"Listen here, smart ass, everyone in this town knows that Jackie is a lying, cheating harlot who's clearly breaking a couple of commandments, but she still gets to teach bible study, so tell me what is it going to hurt to let a bunch of old farts play bingo?" Tandi went to the refrigerator and grabbed out the pickle jar. She unscrewed the top and stabbed a pickle—one that she pointed at me with each word. "I'm telling you, preaching for that man is nothing but a red herring."

"Come Sunday, I am not questioning the preacher or his son."

"Okay, fine, Charlie. But if I were you that's exactly where I would start. Either that or Mike, down at the mechanic's, because what he charges for changing oil should be against the law."

Halfway listening to her, I set the cheese tray on the counter and washed my hands. "Well, I have a plan that doesn't involve going to each member of the town and interrogating them. All I need is a map."

Tandi made a "come hither" motion with her hands. "All right, explain."

"You know, ever since I called you last night, you've really handled all of this rather well."

She stabbed another pickle. "Well, I've always known you had some crazy superhuman powers, but thanks to my Marvel knowledge, I just assumed you were going to start shooting laser beams from your eyes or have blades come out from the back of your hands."

"Sorry to disappoint." I put my hands on my hips. "Let's wait until Jamison gets here and then I'll explain my plan."

"Fine. We'll just practice my lines."

I grumbled, but I still followed her into the living room. She sat down on the couch and patted the cushion next to her, pulling out a white stack of papers and handing them over to me. She tied back her blond hair and did some kind of funny neck exercises, coupled with what I could only imagine to be vocal exercises.

Flipping through the pages she handed me, I sat there waiting patiently while she sounded like a dying donkey. When the braying stopped, I asked, "Why are there words in red ink next to all of your lines?"

"Duh, Scuttle doesn't have a ton of lines, so I just gave him some additional ones."

"Can you do that?"

"Did Cleopatra use her sex appeal as a weapon? The Queen of the Nile knew how to get things done, and she never asked for permission." Tandi's pretty face scrunched up. "Well, come to think of it, she might not be the best example. After all, she did marry a couple of her siblings, and there's no proof she wasn't a product of inbreeding herself, but the girl did know how to wear some eyeliner."

I laughed. Cleopatra couldn't hold a candle to my friend. Only Tandi could take a small part in a play and turn it into a starring role.

"You know I could 'persuade' you to not rehearse your lines."

She clapped her hands. "Oh, I like. I like it a lot. You think you can do the same thing to me as you did with Brandon. By the way, it's hilarious how he's almost scared of you."

Maybe to her but that night totally freaked me out in more ways than one. "I was kidding, Tandi. I'm not going to use my powers on you. What if I screw up?"

She jumped up and ran to the kitchen, only to come back with a large tub of coffee ice cream. "Ugh, I really hate this kind but desperate times and all that. I'm going to eat this on your white couch. There's a possibility I might drop some and when Jamison comes over, he'll either think you're a messy housekeeper, or you crapped on the couch."

I shook my head as she popped the lid and dug a spoonful out. I pointed a finger at her. "Do not eat that bite!"

She not only ate that bite but the next. "Seriously? Put your back into it; this is killing my diet."

Tandi had never been on a diet in her life. I concentrated as hard as I could, commanding her to put the ice cream back in the fridge. I finally gave up when she was halfway through the tub. Eventually, she put the ice cream back by her own free will. I was completely stumped as to why it didn't work on her. I filed the mystery under "things to ask Jamison." Maybe what happened with Brandon was an isolated incident.

chapter eight

Tandi was back on the couch, saying, "Red leather, yellow leather" over and over until I wanted to rip my ears off. My nerves were already bad, and my stomach was doing this little rollercoaster thing every time I thought about Jamison's conversation last night. He spoke the truth. This I knew.

When the doorbell rang, Tandi screeched from the sofa, "I got it."

A minute later, Jamison strolled into the kitchen, looking breathtaking with his faded jeans hanging low on his hips and his signature black T-shirt pulled tight across his chest. How different Talon was with his hair product and name-brand clothes. I sighed. Why was I comparing the two on an appearance level? I chose to stay here and train because it was the best thing for me, not because my trainer was magnificent to look at. Tandi was laughing at something Jamison said. I shook my head in dismay at how easily Tandi had taken a liking to Jamison. Usually, Tandi wasn't so trusting of strangers.

Jamison's eyes did a slow perusal over my body. When his gaze met mine, he said, "You look stunning tonight."

I willed myself not to blush at his cocky smile; I realized my will was crap. Tandi sashayed into the kitchen after him, more like a regal queen than a sidekick. "Hey," then I immediately cringed. That was the best that I could do?

One side of his mouth tilted up. Great. He could probably sense my discomfort. "I thought maybe you could show me how you found that little boy. We could start there, and then before I leave tonight, I would like to talk about the powers you've exhibited so far. Then hopefully tomorrow, you'll be able to reenact everything you've already done."

I didn't have a lot of confidence that I would be able to demonstrate anything but I nodded anyway.

"I picked up a new phone today." He pulled out a new iPhone and swiped the screen a couple of times. "I had my brother send me a picture of the key that he has. Would you like to see it?"

"Yes, that might help." He handed me the phone, and I studied the picture. The key wasn't what I imagined at all. It was the size and shape of a tennis ball but black. There was nothing about it that looked like an actual key. "This is it?"

"Yes. The key actually can separate into two halves, but it has to be together to open up a portal." He laid his phone down on the counter. "Now, tell me how you found this little boy."

I sat down on one of the barstools. Tandi gave me an encouraging nod as I gathered my thoughts. "I've noticed, especially here of late, that the stronger my emotions are, the more chance I have of something weird happening."

"Like the fog, ice, and fire?"

"Yeah, and don't forget persuasion. I persuaded Brandon to forget about me. My emotions were running all over the place the night Colby went missing.

"Tell me about that night."

"My worry amplified when it started getting dark outside. Colby is afraid of the dark and by this point, he had been missing for more than twelve hours. The whole town had broken off into small groups. I kept saying to myself 'I'm going to find him.' The next thing I know, I was telling our small group I wanted to go west instead of east. No one argued… maybe I unknowingly persuaded them, but they followed me as we crossed a small creek bed and an hour later, we found Colby. He was scared but okay."

Tandi added, "It was like she knew exactly where he was. Like there was an imaginary string tying her to Colby. She followed the string and never once wavered off the path."

"The adults in the group were amazed; some even said that one day, I would be a great mom with the intuition that I had. Others said that it made sense that Colby was there because no one else had checked that far west. But I knew that it had something to do with me being different."

He looked satisfied with my story. His long fingers drummed the countertop. "You have no emotional ties to this key, so I'm not expecting you to find it, but I would like for you to try."

"Before I try, can I ask you a question?"

"Of course."

"The woman that you're close with, Ariana, why wouldn't she just tell you who has the key?"

He spun his phone around on the counter. "That's a good question. I think it's because there were a couple of things she wanted me to accomplish while I was here. If I came just for the key, then the other things that she wants to happen might not."

It must be great being a psychic. "Other things? Like what?"

"I'm not completely sure yet."

Hm. Either he did know, or he just didn't want to share. "All right, I'm going to picture the key and tell myself that I really want to find it." And I truly did. If this key could open up portals to beings that were evil, then I needed to make sure it didn't fall in the wrong hands. I had the image in my mind and repeated my desire to find it. I waited for that magnetic pull I felt with Colby but nothing happened. I didn't even want to move off the barstool, much less out of the kitchen to search for it. After another five minutes of trying, I knew it wasn't working.

My eyes opened and focused on Jamison. "I'm sorry. I really did want to help you."

He gave me a smile. "I honestly didn't think it would be this easy. We will find it when the time is right."

Tandi was rubbing her frown line. "Well, darlin', maybe we should find you an operating manual. There has to be some kind of book you could refer to or something?"

Jamison laughed. "I'll be her manual. She will get the hang of all of this before you know it."

Tandi beamed at the both of us like she was picturing our wedding day. "Well, kids, I hate to break up Scooby-Doo and the gang, but I need to study for my physics test."

My brows furrowed. "Since when are you studying physics?"

She grabbed up her jacket and bag, all while avoiding eye contact with me, which was normally what she did when she was lying. "Well, it was a last-minute decision, you know, like a late add-on. But the truth is, you can never have too much knowledge when it comes to, you know, matter and energy and stuff." At my blank look, she said, "All right, well, I gotta go. See y'all later."

After she left, I said, "Well, that was awkward."

"Not for me. Even though I'm sorry your buffer left, I personally wouldn't mind some alone time with you." And he just called me out. "How about we talk about those flaws, as you like to call them?"

He grabbed my hand and led me to the couch. We sat, semi-facing one another.

"The night that you produced the fog, what happened?"

I picked at my cardigan as I recalled that night. "It was the night I had broken up with Brandon." What I didn't say was the reason why. Brandon was pressuring me to do things that I didn't want to do. "I decided to spend the night with Tandi. I had a dream that I had disappeared to somewhere that held no misery, hardships, or heartache. I awoke to her shaking me in a room full of fog."

"What about the ice?"

"The day after my eighteenth birthday, I went to visit my parents' grave. I was an emotional wreck. Tandi came over with a box of tissues and a coffee. When she handed me the coffee, I somehow turned it to ice. When I created the fire, I was looking through a family photo album."

"Then you persuaded your ex to leave you alone."

I nodded. "Oh, but earlier tonight, I tried to persuade Tandi, and it didn't work, and I really tried. I don't understand."

"Well, either you didn't mean what you were asking her to do, or Tandi has a little supernatural in her. If that's the case, it's so diluted that I can't sense it, but anything is possible. Do you think you can try and create fog, right now? That's a pretty safe element. One that won't burn the whole house down."

"Ha! Well, honestly, I don't think I could create anything right now. My emotions aren't running rampant."

"You will have to learn how to call on your powers without using emotions, but we can start that way if we have to. This is what we're going to do. I'm going to kiss you."

My eyes betrayed me as they fell to his lips. "What? Why?"

"Just to get your emotions going, of course." He raked his teeth over his bottom lip. "I'm not kissing you because when you walk in the room, that's all I think about."

My breath hitched at his words. He leaned in slowly, giving me all the time in the world to tell him no. But apparently, I had forgotten how to speak English. He tilted my chin up, and then he kissed me. It was just a brush of lips at first and then the kiss turned into something different. It was sweet with an underlining sense of urgency that I'd never felt before. It was as if this was my first real kiss.

My hair lifted from the back of my neck, and my shirt billowed in the wind. Wait. What wind? Jamison pulled back from me as we both watched the chandelier above us swinging.

"Interesting. You've created wind." He ran a thumb over my bottom lip. "It sounds to me like the fog was from your need to hide, ice was coming from a place of grievance, fire was your anger, and the wind…" His eyes danced with wicked delight. "Well, that was from passion."

"Passion? You think a lot about yourself." I blushed when he arched an eyebrow. "Okay, maybe I did enjoy the kiss." Maybe was the understatement of the year. "But what teenager wouldn't like kissing an attractive male?"

"Attraction. Passion. Call it what you want, but it still made this," he said as he pointed to the dying wind. "Most witches can call on one element. You can call up four elements, plus you have the ability to persuade, and who knows what other tricks you might have up your sleeve? First, we need to figure out how to control the elements, and then we will work on calling them up without relying on your emotions."

The second kiss completely took me off guard. His hand reached out and snagged me behind the neck quicker than I could process. His lips were on mine again. There was no denying the sensations I felt head to toe were hot, relentless passion. Everything in my being wanted him to never stop.

The crystals on the chandelier clinked together. I felt his lips smile against mine. I pulled back enough to see his blue eyes swirling into a beautiful honey color, showing me a beast lying just beneath the surface. I should have been afraid, but I found myself more enthralled.

"I love wind," he said. "I wanted to see it again."

I rolled my eyes and was trying to think of something to say that wasn't stupid when the phone rang.

chapter nine

On the fourth ring, I answered. "Hello?"

"Hey, beautiful, I was wondering if you wanted to get together for lunch tomorrow?" Talon's overly charming voice was not loud by any means, but I knew the werewolf I had just been kissing could hear the conversation with no problem.

I turned my back to Jamison, trying to create more privacy. Not that it would help. "Listen, this training camp sounds amazing, but I think right now the best decision is for me to stick close to my loved ones while I try to straighten out the kinks. And, I'm working on how to control this new side of me."

Talon was silent for a moment. "I heard that my old pal, Jamison, was in town. He wouldn't be the one helping you with your power, would he?"

I looked to Jamison for guidance. He gave me a curt nod, so I replied, "Actually, yes, he is."

"Are you what has brought him to town?"

Something in my gut tightened. I'd learned over the years to trust my gut more than anything else, and right now my intuition told me to keep quiet. It's not that I

wanted to lie to Talon, but I knew that if Jamison had any chance of finding the key, he needed to be secretive. I mean, he had a world to save—one that I was currently inhabiting. Not to mention, I had made a promise to Jamison. "Yeah. Apparently, I've been projecting to the world that I can't control my powers, so he came to help out."

"Out of the goodness of his heart, I'm sure."

"You've both been very nice."

Talon was so silent on the other end of the line that for a second, I thought we had lost the connection. Finally, he said, "That's unfortunate. I was hoping that we would get to know one another on a more personal level. Before I go tomorrow, I would still like to take you to lunch."

"Um, yeah, sure." Why in the world did I agree to that? Spending more time with Talon on any level was the last thing that I wanted to do.

"Great. See you tomorrow."

"At Ma's diner?"

"Sounds great. I look forward to it."

After saying goodbye, I hung up the phone. Drawing up my composure, I turned around to find Jamison scowling. "What?"

"I don't like him."

"So you've said. Want to elaborate?"

Jamison sat on the couch. Leaning forward, he rested his elbows on his knees. "I don't have proof, but I think Talon has been working for the Degenerates."

"That's a pretty heavy accusation."

"You asked, and I told you my opinion." His tone was stiff. "Why are you meeting him tomorrow?"

I got that he didn't like Talon but there was more to this. He sounded… jealous. Testing the waters, I said, "Because he offered me something when I thought I needed it the most. And I don't like to burn bridges. One day, I might decide to go to his training camp."

Jamison's jaw clenched. "I can't tell you what to do, but I can say I don't think that would be a good idea."

"Your opinion has been noted. Now, are we done for the night, or is there anything else that you think I can accomplish?"

"Oh, there is a lot more that you can do. I believe you'll be able to turn any form of liquid into ice, turn objects into ash, and surround yourself with wind and fog before it's all said and done. I also believe you will be able to persuade the weakest of supernaturals to do anything you want. But control is not something you learn in a night."

"I'll only be able to persuade the weak?"

"What is something that you want right now?"

For him to kiss me again, but I couldn't say that. "Ben and Jerry's double fudge ice cream."

He laughed as his eyes were fixated on my face. The intensity in his gaze makes my face warm. "You didn't even have to think about that one. I sense a hidden addiction somewhere in there." He patted the couch seat next to him. After I sat back down, he looked me in the eyes. "Make me go to the store and get you some. Try to persuade me like you did Brandon and attempted to do with Tandi. Think about how badly you wanted Brandon to leave you alone. Use that same desire, need, and want, apply it to how badly you want the ice cream, and then tell me to go get it."

I did just as he asked. I pictured the ice cream that I wanted and my desire for him to get it for me. I shoved the image towards him. "Go get me some ice cream now, please."

His head turned to the side. "Good job. I felt you pushing in on my thoughts, so that means Tandi must have some supernatural in her. Though it's diluted so much, it would never amount to anything."

I found myself frowning. "I hate it didn't work on you."

He chucked me under the chin. "I said the weak, love. There is nothing about me that is weak. Besides, you don't need to persuade me to do anything. After we create wind a couple more times, I'll probably be wrapped around your pinky so tight you could make me jump off the tallest bridge just by batting those pretty eyelashes."

I couldn't help the laugh escaping my lips. We discussed my ability to create fog, and after a couple more hours of concentrating hard on my emotions, I was able to create a small puff. It looked more like a smoke ring then it did fog, but Jamison seemed to be delighted at my progress. He was a patient, kind teacher, and I had to mentally slap myself several times to keep myself from sighing out loud. At ten we finally said our goodbyes. I was secretly hoping for another kiss and was a little disappointed when it didn't come. I locked the door behind him and trudged up to my bedroom. I tossed and turned in bed. There was something about Jamison that just didn't add up. The guy looked like he had fallen from heaven, had a charming personality, and was confident, but there was something big that I wasn't seeing. My gut told me I could trust him. It also told me that I was safe with him. So why did I feel like he was hiding something from me? Maybe the answer was right in front of me but because I'm more than a little infatuated, I'm missing it. Sometimes when things were too good to be true, people were left feeling disappointed. I hoped Jamison wouldn't be a disappointment.

After a sleepless night, I threw on some clothes and dragged my feet down the stairs. All night I had dreams of blue eyes swirling with honey. I had barely had time to finish my cereal when Tandi showed up. She strode in wearing a hot pink blazer, tight jeans, and pearls. The girl was always in pearls.

She snapped her fingers. "Coffee. I need coffee," she said as she headed over to make her cup.

"Umm, good morning. Are you driving me to school today?" Totally missed that memo.

"Yes. I had to come by to see how last night went." After she had her steaming cup of coffee in her hands, she sat next to me. "All right, spill the beans. Tell me how it went last night after I left."

I rolled my eyes at her. "Tandi, he knew that you didn't have a physics class. I don't know what you were thinking."

"I thought that three was a crowd. A wheel that you didn't need."

"Well, nothing happened." I bit my lip. "Well, maybe a little something happened."

Her eyes widened. "Don't you leave me hanging. I want all the details."

I explained to her about the phone call I received from Talon and then about Jamison's kisses that I still couldn't put out of my mind.

Tandi squealed. "I knew it! I just knew that he was your soul mate. I can sense these things."

"You're crazy. He is not my anything. But I need to be honest with you. Even though that kiss was electrifying, there is something about him that is off."

"Like Ted Bundy off, or like he's hiding that he has a secret sweet tooth?"

"He's definitely hiding something, but it's more than just a need for candy." Trust is such a precious thing. It was something that I instinctively shy away from and yet I trust Jamison even though I know he is hiding something.

Tandi patted my knee. "But you do like him?"

I think of the way he makes me feel when he's around and instead offer my bestie an easier answer. "What's not to like?"

"Truth. So you've decided to let the angel train you here, and Face will now be heading back to wherever it is he's from?"

I thought about Talon. There was definitely something he was hiding, too.

"Right. Starting today, I'm going to learn how to control all the elements that I seem to wield when my emotions are high, but we still have to keep it a secret."

"Um, duh. What are you so afraid of? That I'll share your freaky self with the world? Have I ever told anyone anything you didn't want me to? No, never."

"Well, now, that's not entirely true."

Tandi looked shocked. "I have never."

I nodded. "Yes, you have. Remember that time we were in first grade and Bobby Jenkins kept pulling my pigtails so hard my eyes watered. He stole my lunch money every day. He pushed me off of the merry-go-round. He would trip me when I walked by. I put up with his bullying for weeks, and when I confided in you, I swore you to secrecy."

"Ah, now I remember, but I don't think that really counts as telling your secrets."

I laughed. "You went and got my brother, Wes, and told him that if he didn't take care of Bobby Jenkins, you'd follow him around everywhere he went calling him your lover boy and embarrass him in front of all his friends."

With a smile, she said, "If I remember correctly, your hot brother beat the crap out of Bobby Jenkins."

"I think that's probably more because he was scared about your threat of sticking to him like glue and less about his love for me."

"That's not true. Your brother has always been there for you."

Wes was only two years older than me, but he jumped into the role of loving parent and didn't bat an eye. He was supposed to be home in two more weeks. Sometime last night when I was tossing and turning, I decided to tell my brother about my flaws. Now that I had help on handling what was happening to me, I knew I wouldn't be a burden to him.

chapter ten

alon was in the back booth at Ma's Diner with his back to the entrance. I had to make this quick and return to school before our lunch break was over. As I approached him, I heard him on his cell phone. "That's right. Let's go ahead and put the plan into motion."

I slid into the booth opposite of him, and he smiled at me. He put up one finger, telling me to give him a minute. After a few seconds, he finally hung up. "Sorry about that. When you're in charge, you never get a break, even for a beautiful girl."

Shifting uncomfortably in my seat, I tried to smile. "So you're leaving today to go to…?"

"Sorry, I can't tell you the location. It's for security purposes. I'm sure there are a lot of people that would like to get their hands on a whole bunch of weak supernaturals in training. Some of those kids haven't even learned the basics. They would be like sitting ducks."

"Oh, well, that makes sense." I studied the boy in front of me. He looked tired. Maybe he got as little sleep as I did last night.

We ordered some lunch, and for the most part, I just sat there letting him talk about the training camp. He was ambitious, and it showed. To be as young as him and be a leader was amazing. Then it occurred to me that looks could be deceiving. Jamison appeared to be twenty.

"Talon, how old are you?"

"Nineteen, why?"

I pushed my empty plate away. "It's just you never know. People can look nineteen but be three hundred and nineteen."

His brief smile showed perfectly even, straight teeth. "How many supernaturals have you met?"

"Just one other than you."

His smile dropped. "Oh, so we're talking about Jamison?"

I didn't know what their deal was, but it was apparent there wasn't much love between them.

After a couple of awkward moments of silence, he asked, "Since you're finished with your food, do you mind if I put a bubble around us, so there will be no eavesdropping?"

"No, go ahead."

With a wave of his hand, our table was completely soundproof. The air around us shimmered. Such a cool trick. Talon rapped his knuckles a couple of times on the table like he was weighing his words before speaking. "The power that you cast out a week ago let us know that you're going to be a higher-level witch. Usually, those witches can create an element. Have you discovered which one you will be able to call to you?"

I opened my mouth, but nothing came out. My gut was tightening again, and it always won. For whatever reason, I didn't want to show him all of my cards. Out of the four tricks that I could create, I considered fog to be the least powerful. "I can call fog but not intentionally."

He looked a little confused with my answer. "One of my people saw the energy you were releasing. They talked of it as a great power. Don't get me wrong; fog is a great trick to have, but are you sure that's it?"

"I'm positive. I fell asleep one night, and when I awoke, I was surrounded by fog."

He mulled over my answer. There was no doubt that disappointment colored his face. "Maybe they were wrong." He reached across the table. He hesitated for a second before his hand grabbed mine. "Is there nothing that I can do to change your mind about coming with me?"

At his touch, my gut screamed for me to put some distance between us. I very awkwardly disentangled my hand from his. Talon made me uncomfortable, and I was pretty sure it was showing. "I'm guessing if my power is a lower level one, there is not a whole lot of training that I will need. I don't know what I would bring to your camp."

"Your beauty would cheer everyone up."

I smiled. "Thanks, but I think I'm going to stay here."

We said our goodbyes and then with one final wave, I watched Talon get in a sporty car and drive off. I turned to head back to my car, and saw Jamison standing under an old tree, silently watching Talon's taillights fade in the distance. What in the world was he doing? Was he spying on me? I crossed the street. When I was two feet from him, his gaze swiveled to me.

My eyebrows rose in question. "Um, well, this isn't creepy at all."

He shrugged. "I don't trust him."

"I didn't ask. Were you standing there the whole time, watching us through the diner window?"

"What did he say? Did he ask about your powers?"

Ugh! "You are crossing a line, bud. Lunch is over. I'm going back to class."

Jamison grabbed hold of my hand, stopping me in my tracks. I looked up at him, and my breath almost caught. He was so damn hot it was hard to even remember how to breathe. He pulled me close to him where I could feel his hard stomach muscles underneath his T-shirt.

"I'm sorry that you're mad, but I'm not sorry I was making sure you're okay. Talon is up to something, and I don't like it."

Concentrate, Charlie. My voice came out raspy. "If I knew the history that you two shared, then maybe I would understand where you're coming from. It's obviously something more than you think he's working for the Degenerates. Do you want to tell me about it?"

He gave me a small frown before he released me. Now, I was the one disappointed. "Can you miss the rest of your classes?"

I hadn't missed a day all year, so I would be fine. When the school called my brother, he would call me to see why I missed some classes. I guess I could tell him I was exhausted. Technically, that wasn't a lie, considering how this past week had gone. "What did you have in mind?"

"Take a ride with me?"

Something about his tone made me want to go with him. It was as if he was begging. "Sure."

We walked in silence to his Jeep Wrangler. After he held my door open for me, I got in and sent a quick text to Tandi, letting her know I was going with Jamison. All I needed was her putting out an APB on her missing friend.

He turned down a road and after a few minutes, I knew where he was headed. The only thing down this road was an old farm with a dilapidated plantation house still standing between some old oak trees. When the beauty came into view, I couldn't help but smile. It was two stories, white, and massive, with a traditional, Southern wrap-around porch. The wooden shutters hung askew, and vines crept up the sides of the house. I'd always loved this house and hated how it had fallen into such disrepair.

He pulled off the side of the road, and we both exited the jeep and started walking in the mile-high grass. "There is something about this place that calls to me."

"Yeah, it's sad and beautiful at the same time."

"Just like when I met you. You were sad and stunningly beautiful." I turned my head, so he didn't see me blush. "History can be sad, too. But like this house, its history has made it what it is." We walked up the abandoned porch steps. He flicked a piece of peeling paint. "It's weathered the storm and has the scars to show for it, but it hasn't crumbled."

We both sat on a porch swing, and I held my breath when it groaned under our weight. When it didn't come crashing down, I smiled. "Tell me your history."

He grabbed my hand, placing it on his thigh. My body tingled at the contact and I could feel it spreading quickly all the way down to my toes. A corner of his lip curled up, and I knew it was because of those stupid pheromones. They were leaking out of my body before I was touching his thigh. If my lust could just take a backseat for a moment that would be flipping fantastic. "You know how the Lux had all seven keys at one time? Some say they were taken because the Lux weren't powerful enough to keep them. Some say the Lux got lazy or trusted the wrong people. I tend to think it's somewhere in the middle of all of that. The keys will always be something that are sought after. After all, that was why I was sent here, and I don't know how to feel about that."

"What do you mean?"

"Both of my parents lost their lives because of a key they were entrusted with. My dad was the Werewolf King. He almost flaunted the key, along with his power, because he assumed that no one would be crazy enough to come for it. He was wrong. Because of his misjudgment, both of my parents are dead. Now, I'm here after a key, and I can't help but wonder if it's the one he lost all of those years ago."

I laid my head on his chest. No matter how many years ago his parents were buried, he was still raw over their death. Maybe that was the connection I felt to him? Either way, I could hear the hurt in his voice, and it was killing me.

"The reason I can help you with your powers is because when my mother was unable to have children, she went to Ariana for help. Ariana granted her wish and gave her two boys, but we wouldn't be just werewolves. Mom carried us in her womb but Ariana created us. She gave us powers and senses that belong to other supernaturals. The speed of a vampire, intuition of a witch, and strength of a werewolf. Like I told you earlier, my brother and I are hybrids. In my heart, I believe I won't make the same mistakes as my father. Just because I'm stronger and more powerful than him doesn't mean I can protect the key. His arrogance, trusting the wrong people, and selfishness got him and my mother killed. Being wary of others is what has kept me alive this long. So if I am a little apprehensive of Talon and his need to help, I have my reasons."

My gut reared its ugly head again. "There is more to that story, isn't there?"

He draped an arm around me and kissed the top of my head as I listened to his heartbeat. "I have no proof, but I think it was Talon's uncle who led the rouge werewolves to my parents' house all those years ago."

That was a pretty heavy accusation, but I knew he believed what he was saying. I didn't know if it was fair, though, to blame Talon for his uncle's evil doings. Especially since there was no proof his uncle even committed the crime. "Well, then, I understand why you have reservations about him, but he's leaving today, so that's one less worry you will have. We need to be focusing on finding your key."

"What I'm looking for is dangerous, and there's a good chance that whoever has the key knows I'm here. If you're going to continue to help me find it, you need to tap into your powers and learn to control them so that you can protect yourself." He stood up and offered me a hand. "Do you know what this farm has? More than a hundred acres. This is the perfect place for you to practice."

"Yeah, but even though it's an abandoned property, it's not ours. What if I set the woods on fire?"

He pulled me down the steps. "I actually bought this place today, and since the new owner happens to like you, I think it'll be okay if you practice."

Wait. What? "You bought this place?"

He gave a little shrug as if it was no big deal. Who was this guy? I followed him around the huge house and to an open field. He gave my hand one final squeeze. "Have at it."

Talk about performance anxiety. My hands immediately began to sweat.

"Um, I'm not sure if—"

He gave me a sexy smile. "Tell me you need help creating wind. I would be happy to volunteer my services."

I rolled my eyes and turned my back on him, so I wouldn't be tempted. My hormones were all over the place. With my luck, I would kiss him once, and the wind would be so strong it would bring his newly acquired house down. So, no to wind. But what did I want to create? Or better yet, what did I think I could create?

I walked a small distance to a creek bed running adjacent to the old farmhouse. Kneeling down, I let the water flow over my hand. Creating power the only way I knew how, I let my emotions float to the surface. I closed my eyes and remembered. My parents loved this old farmhouse. They often talked about how if they had enough money, they would buy the property and give it a makeover. Put some horses in the old barn out back. Mom had said she would have a vegetable garden. Man, I missed them terribly. As the first tear trailed down my hand, I heard clapping. Opening my eyes, I saw that I had turned three feet of the creek to ice.

Jamison helped me to my feet. He softly cupped my face in his hands. His lips touched mine in the barest of whispers. "You did well. It hurts when you make ice. I would rather see you make wind." Then he kissed me, and the bite of the wind never felt so good.

chapter eleven

L ater that night, I sat on my couch with Tandi. I
had just gotten off the phone with Wes, who was
in overprotective brother mode. Because I skipped class,
and the school notified him he was all of a sudden
having doubts about leaving his younger sister at home
and wanted to know if I could go stay with Tandi and
her parents until he returned. I politely declined. Tandi's
parents were horrible people. They were rude, arrogant,
and condescending. Yeah, that was a big no thanks. But
I did tell him that I would ask Tandi to spend the night
with me.

After I hung up, she said, "So, you don't think big
brother has powers?" I shook my head. "Which would
mean that one of your parents were human?"

"Yeah, I don't think the starving artist has powers."

"But he's so freaking hot. Like hawt."

"Gross. He's my brother. Cut it out." I threw a couch
pillow at her. "You want to watch a movie?"

"I guess. Are you and Jamison like an established
couple or what?"

"I don't know exactly what we are." Kissing partners? Makers of wind? "I know I think about him way more than I should."

She started to say something when the doorbell rang. I gave her a puzzled look before I got up to answer it. Talon stood there with all of his pretty-boy charms. You have got to be freaking kidding me.

Tandi gave him a finger wave. "Hey, Face. What's up?" She mumbled out of the corner of her mouth, "Stalk much lately?"

One of his eyebrows arched up to his hairline. "Um, hey?"

"I thought you left town already," I said.

"That was the plan, but then I came across someone that used to know your parents, and I figured you probably didn't know who your parents really were, considering you can't control your fog." He gave me a sheepish look. "No offense. Anyways, I came to make you a final offer. Just come and look at the training camp with me. You don't have to stay. I just want you to see what you're going to miss out on." He gave me a wink. "It's the weekend; you won't miss any classes. View the training camp and Juan. He's the guy who knew your parents. I bet he could answer a lot of questions that probably have been swirling around in that head of yours."

My heart leaped in excitement before I realized that Talon was waving a carrot in front of my face and I was the donkey. He came here with a plan and he was hoping I would buy it. Hook, line, and sinker. Would it be an answer to my prayers if this man, Juan, could tell me everything I wanted to know? Absolutely? Does Talon know that? Probably. Would I have answers for Wes when he came home. Yep, and things were always easier to handle when you knew the answers to why things were happening but Talon showing up at my door with promises… too convenient. My gut was telling me that this was my fate though. I needed to go to that camp. So I would pretend to get along with Talon… for the time being. I needed to find out why he was so highly motivated to get me to this camp.

The decision was made. I felt good about it until Tandi said, "Can I come?"

"Sorry. No," Talon said with a shake of his head. "The supernatural community has lots of laws on how humans can't know about us. To be honest, if some of the higher-ups knew that you were privy to some of the stuff that you already know, it wouldn't be good for you Tandi."

Tandi came to stand next to me at the door. "This training camp, it's for witches?"

"Yes."

"So, is there anyone there that can sniff me out?"

"I don't really know what you're—"

Tandi was just too smart for him. She knew that his impromptu visit was shady as hell too. It seems he might've underestimated us both. "I can pretend to be a low-level witch just for the short time we're there?"

I gave my friend a pointed look. "I would prefer that you didn't come."

"Yeah, well I am. So get over it."

I glared at her. This was too dangerous. I didn't want to risk her. "We're not staying the night. We'll go and visit the camp, check the place out, and then talk to Juan. After that, we will come back home."

Poor Talon piped up like he had any say so in the matter. "I guess it's possible she can come with you, as long as she doesn't talk to anyone, but the nearest training facility is more than two hundred miles from here. We wouldn't get there until late tonight, so it wouldn't be until tomorrow when we could have a look at the camp."

I didn't want to stay at his camp, and I definitely didn't trust him but knowledge was everything. My gut was telling me I would find some missing pieces to the puzzle if I went.

I gave him a nod. "Give me the location, and we will meet you there."

He handed me a folded-up piece of paper.

Tandi peered over my shoulder. "Um, it's blank."

"The directions are on the flyer. The paper holds a lot of magic, so only witches can read it."

She rolled her eyes. "Got your own secret society and everything. I need to go and pack an overnight bag. It's one thing if we're staying here. I don't mind sleeping in the nude, but I can't be showing off the goodies to a whole bunch of witches. Swing by and pick me up?"

"Duh."

Tandi gave me a concerned look, and I knew that she had a bad feeling about all of this too, but she was unwilling to let me go by myself. She clapped her hands. "Come on, Face, you can walk me out." She didn't wait for him to follow her.

Talon shook his head. "Why does she call me Face?" I just shrugged. "Okay, so I'll see you later tonight?"

"Yes. Tell Juan to be ready."

I watched both of them hop into their cars before I shut the door. I didn't have time to make it up the stairs to pack my own bag before there was a knock on the door. What now?

I was a little shocked to see Jamison on the other side. He didn't wait for an invitation; he just strolled right in. "Before you ask me if I was spying, I was. When I realized that Talon hadn't left town like he originally told you, I started following him around."

"He came back because—"

He waved a hand. "Yes, yes, I heard. Great hearing, remember? This is a trap. You can't go."

"Yes, I know."

He talked right over me. "Think about it," he said, pacing in my living room. "This town isn't that big. I have picked up on no other supernaturals other than Talon. Ariana sent me here, so we also know that the key is here, but who has it? He has to be the one. And I know that you want information about your parents, but have you thought about why he wants you so badly?"

Talon thought that I could make fog. A pretty useless gift when it came to creating elements. Unless he knew that I lied. But I think there is something we are missing. That's why I need to go.

"You didn't hear me. I agree with you. I think this is a lure of some sort."

That got his attention. He stopped pacing as a scowl appeared on his face. "Then why the hell would you agree to go?" Honey swirled in his blue eyes. His beast wasn't happy either.

"Because there are answers that I need." Not to mention that it felt right to go. Dang gut better not be faulty. "Why do you think he wants me so badly?"

"I think it's because he knows you're my—" His words were cut off as he just gave me a blank stare.

"I'm your what?" He sighed, and I knew he wasn't going to finish his sentence. Was he going to say girlfriend? What was the big deal? Did he have commitment issues? I found myself getting mad. My hands heated but I ignored them. If he didn't want to be my boyfriend, then why was he constantly hanging out with me? Kissing me? Was I just another girl?

"You know what? I'm going. Whatever his reasons are, I'll find them out eventually."

"Did you not hear me? I think he has the key. Which means he is—"

A cloud of gray fog swirled in the middle of my living room. The fog was coming from someone, but it wasn't me. As quickly as it came, it disappeared. An old woman stood five feet in front of me. She had long, thin, grey hair and a wrinkled face that put her age somewhere between Ebenezer Scrooge and Methuselah. If I had to guess, I would say she was at least a hundred years past the date of her death. Maybe she was a zombie. Her completely white eyes rolled to me. Was she blind?

I started to wave a hand in front of her face when Jamison asked, "Ariana, what are you doing here?"

There went my zombie theory.

She shuffled her feet to him. "Would you believe I just missed you?"

He gathered her up in a hug. "No, Noni, I wouldn't."

"Then I guess it doesn't matter what I have to say." She turned towards me. "And this is the beautiful Charlize. It is a pleasure to meet you, child."

I was still weirded out, but I found myself extending a hand. "Nice to meet you, too. Jamison has spoken highly of you."

She laughed. "That's because he knows I would know if he didn't." Jamison gave her an endearing smile filled with love. "I needed to pop over and give some advice."

"Let me guess, I was veering off the path?"

"You mean if you actually went through with your plan of tying her to a chair until she agreed to listen to reason, then, yes, you would have definitely stepped off the path."

My mouth dropped open. "You were thinking about keeping me a prisoner in my own home?"

"That can't be proven." He looked over at Ariana. "Tell me that you came here to reason with her."

"Sorry, my dear boy. She needs to go. It's part of her destiny. Everything will change if she does not go tonight, and not for the better. I can promise you I will be unable to fix what the outcome will be. So yes, she must go." She straightened her hunched shoulders to the best of her ability, as if she was gearing up for a fight. "And she must do it without you."

"What? No! You've lost your mind."

"I know what you're thinking. I see far and wide. This is the only way. You can slay someone's dragons, or you can teach them to slay." She patted his cheek. "Nothing will happen to your—your friend. I'm sure you will think of a way to keep tabs on her should she need your assistance."

The woman turned to me once again. "Find your powers, child, and wield them to win the battle and help find the key." Her eyes darted left to right. "Hold on... something is coming in." What was she talking about? After a couple of seconds, she said, "Sorry, the Undertaker is keeping me on my toes. I have to go. Charlie, you control your emotions. They don't control you. Remember that."

"It was nice meeting—" Fog quickly circled around Ariana, and she disappeared from my house as quickly as she'd entered.

Jamison stood there, clenching his jaw. I walked around him and up the steps to pack a bag, knowing he would follow me. "Look, my gut is telling me that you believe Talon has the key, but isn't that what we're looking for?"

He stood in the doorway while I shoved some clothes into a duffel bag. "I don't like this at all. If Ariana says you will be fine, then you will be, but that doesn't mean that I have to like it. She also hinted that I should mark you."

I stopped packing. "Was that attached to the group email because I must have missed the memo. When did she say that, and what do you mean by mark?"

"She said I would find a way to you if you needed my help. The only way I can do that is by marking you." He came into the room. "This might just save you and your friend's life."

I had more to worry about than just myself. I couldn't bring Tandi into a dangerous situation without a plan. "What do I need to do?"

"I'm going to bite you on your shoulder blade. It won't hurt, and no one will be able to see the mark unless they are a werewolf. It connects us on a deeper level. It's how my kind become mated."

"Mated?"

"Sort of like how humans get married. But we won't be mated unless we vow to be each other's mate now and forever. Also, we would have to mingle our blood together. So I can promise you this is just one step in a process, so we won't be mated."

My gut roared to life with that one word. Mated. Heat swirled in my abdomen and spread throughout my body. "How long will I have the mark for?"

He gave a shrug that wasn't too reassuring. "Does it really matter?" When I didn't say anything, he threw up both hands in aggravation. "How about as soon as Ariana tells me to, I will have it removed?"

Something told me not to fight this. "Well, then, in that case, mark away."

He closed the distance between us in two steps. He draped my hair to one side and twined his large hand into my locks as they hung over my shoulder. At his light touch, goose bumps popped up all over my arms. He pulled my sweater along with my bra strap down my shoulder.

I watched in fascination as his canines lengthened. His lips kissed me above my collar bone right before he bit down. I felt a sharp stinging sensation before my body grew warm all over. Towards the end, I was almost purring as he let me go.

He smiled down at me like he was about to devour me, and some part of me knew that if he tried, I would let him, so I took a step back until my legs hit the bed. "You lied. You said it wouldn't hurt."

His smile dropped. "Did it hurt?"

"Only right at first."

"Sorry. I didn't know that it would hurt because you are the first person I've ever marked."

My belly tightened at his words. "Oh." I moved around him to go look in the vanity mirror. I studied my shoulder. "I can't see a thing."

He came to stand behind me. His finger traced an outline of something. "I can. It's my wolf's mark. They are like zebra stripes. They are all different. The edges of the mark are light blue, and the center is a golden hue."

I made contact with his eyes in the mirror. "The two shades are like your eyes then. Light blue until you start to transform, and then they become like honey."

"I guess so." His head bent as he gave my shoulder another quick kiss. "When you have really strong emotions, I'll be able to find you no matter where you are. Unless you burn the whole place down before I can get to you."

"Ha. Ha. Funny." I turned to face him. "You're attracted to me?"

His hands gripped me by my hips. "What kind of question is that? You know I am."

"I'm just trying to figure this out." Us out. "You're attracted to me, you're clearly worried about me leaving tonight, yet I could have sworn that earlier when you couldn't finish your sentence, it was because you were having a hard time with the word 'girlfriend.'"

He gave a little laugh. "So, that is what prompted the sparks of fire from the fingertips?" I must've been too mad to notice. He softly kissed my forehead, nose, and then my lips. "Charlie, you are so much more than that."

His touch was possessive as one hand cradled the back of my neck. His lips met mine, and warm heat rippled through my body. The mark he gave me throbbed as his tongue intertwined with mine. When he finally released me, my breath was ragged, my chest rising and falling.

I was still trying to get my bearings as he walked over to my duffel bag, zipping it. He threw it over his shoulder. "I don't want to let you go." After that kiss, I was tempted to stay. "Come on. I'll walk you to your car."

I locked up the house and after getting in my car, I waved goodbye to him. As I drove to pick up Tandi, I thought about what was to come. Everything about Talon and this camp felt off. I had those feelings before, but now they were stronger. A ton of things with Talon didn't add up. And maybe he did have the key. If so, I would gather as much information as possible, do some behind-the-scenes recon, and then give everything I knew about where it was located to Jamison. Even if I learned nothing new about my parents, this trip wouldn't be a total waste of time if I garnered information about the key. My gut didn't flinch when Ariana said I would be fine. What could possibly go wrong?

chapter twelve

We pulled up to the address around midnight. I was a nervous wreck. My gut was screaming run. If this was the path I was supposed to be on, then I sure as heck didn't want to be on the wrong one. Jeez. It looked like we had landed ourselves on some B-rated movie scene for a generic cable channel. All our surroundings needed was some blonde chick attempting to run, but instead found herself tripping over leaves, while the killer in the ski mask stood perfectly still and yet somehow managed to catch up to her. This place was a dump. Trash littered the forest and a metal spray-painted sign warned trespassers they would be shot. We were literally in the middle of the swamp, where only the very poor or the very strong survived.

"You know," Tandi said, "the term 'ride or die' is overused and not meant to be taken literally." I parked the car in the woods. There was a small trail we would have to hike up to get where the flyer said the camp was located. "You know the part in the scary movie when you're like 'girl don't do it' and then she does it? There is a narrator in my head right now saying, 'and the girls decided to go into the creepy woods, even though their mothers raised them better.' All we need is a guy with a chainsaw and some banjo music."

"It is scary how we're thinking the exact same thing. I've got the same feeling. Dig deep, my friend. Find your lady balls and let's get this night over with. Remember not to say anything to anyone."

Tandi hooked her arm through mine as we walked the dark trail with no light other than what little my cellphone was providing. Finally, we saw a campfire. As branches snapped underneath our feet, everyone gathered outside quit talking and began to stare at us.

Talon met us in the open clearing. "Ladies. We've been partying a little. Prematurely celebrating your arrival. Would either of you care for a beer?" Tandi shook her head, and I declined as well. "There is plenty if either of you should change your mind. Come on. Let me introduce you both."

He placed a hand on either of our backs and steered us around the campfire. All the boys leered, and the girls either acted snotty or indifferent. Some gave us body scans and the others turned their backs on us. Great group of kids. Their mothers must be super proud. The knot in my gut tightened. I looked at our surroundings, trying to get a lay of the land. Several shacks were scattered throughout the woods.

Talon caught me studying them. "This is where our witches in training live. Sort of like dorms."

Dorms where? In a third world country? I seriously doubted there was electricity or running water. "But this isn't where you are staying. If you would like, I can show you both where you will be living."

Living? We were here for the night. His voice was a little slurred, and he reeked of beer, so I let the comment slide as my stomach churned with worry. My gut was telling me that danger hung in every corner and I needed to tread lightly. We took a different path leading us farther away from the campfire. I knew Tandi was apprehensive, and the truth was I was starting to doubt Ariana and my gut.

A man with caramel skin was walking towards us. His head was held high as if he was striding through a royal court not a snake-infested forest. "Hello, Talon. Is this her?"

Talon tried to stand taller. The man was someone he obviously wanted to impress. "I thought you would be in bed by now. I told her earlier she would have to wait to meet you tomorrow."

"Nonsense," the older man said. "She has come all this way. I don't mind talking to her tonight."

Talon shrugged. "Oh, okay. Well this is Tandi, and this is—"

The man who appeared to be in his forties cut Talon off. "I know who this is. The only other person I've ever met with violet eyes was Caro."

"My mother," I whispered.

He gave me a smile. "Come with me. I'm sure you have lots of questions."

My gut flared with warnings as the three of us followed him to a cabin that was pretty luxurious compared to the shacks. There was a generator outside that gave his cabin light. We entered and were ushered to the living room. "My name is Juan, and I am the commander here. I was more than happy when Talon reported back to me about you. When I heard your last name, Galloway, I had my suspicions, but they were confirmed when he described you to me. You are a beauty just like your mother was. Shame what happened to her and your father. I take it you get your name from him?"

I looked over at Tandi briefly. She was taking all of this in, like showing up to a cabin in the woods and talking a stranger about the past, really well. The only sign she gave that she was nervous was one of her legs bouncing up and down.

"Um, yeah. My dad's name was Charles. So they named me Charlize and over the years, my family and friends gave me the nickname Charlie." Feeling a little impatient, I said, "What can you tell me about them?"

Juan sat in the chair opposite of the couch that Talon, Tandi, and I sat on. One finger tapped his chin. "I'm assuming you want to know about what they hid from you?" At my nod, he said, "Your mother was a very powerful witch. I'm not sure if you know this, but most witches usually have only one power they can wield, but thanks to her heritage, she had multiple elements she could control. Wind, fire, water, just to name a few."

"Her heritage?"

Juan gave me a smile. "Sorry. I forget how little you know. Yes, Devon, your mother's father—who would've been your grandfather—was the Warlock King. Upon his death, the crown fell to his only child, your mother; however, she never claimed it. It seemed that she had gone missing, and no witch or warlock could find her, though they valiantly tried. Now, we know she wasn't missing, but she was hiding. The question is why? Why would she want to live amongst the humans when she could wear a crown?"

Talon patted me on the knee. "We think that either she didn't want the responsibility of being Queen of Witches and Warlocks, or she had something to hide. Something like you."

"Me?" I croaked. "Why would she want to hide me?"

Juan crossed his legs at the knees. "That's the question we have been asking since we've found out about you. It has come to our attention that we know little about your father. We are unsure of exactly what he was. If we knew that, maybe it would shine some light on the situation." Arrogance leaked out of his every pore. "If you stayed here at the training camp, we could monitor you and find the answers together. Also, you need to take into consideration that the crown has been in limbo with no one worthy to wear it, but with Caro's long-lost daughter returned to the warlock and witch community, everyone expects you to claim the crown."

Dread pooled deep in my stomach and I was two seconds from bugging out. These were not the pieces to the puzzle that I expected to find in coming here. You didn't have to have the best intuition in the world to know that Juan was not an upstanding citizen. My gut was telling me to remain calm.

"You won't be able to keep it for too long, though," Talon said, "if your powers aren't substantial. The only way someone can take the crown is if they challenge royalty—

you. And with fog being your only element that will be a fight you won't win. You will lose the crown before you have a chance to wear it."

My head was reeling in bewilderment. My grandfather was a ruler? My mother who loved to bake cookies on Sunday mornings was supposed to have been a queen? And now they want me to wear a crown… the family crown. A crown that is just a symbol of power. Power that I'm not able to control. I will wield this so-called power for whose gain? What was his angle?

"Whoa. I don't want to fight anyone." I didn't want the crown if it meant that I would be in leagues with Juan and Talon. "All I want is some answers and to figure out how to control my ability."

Tandi scooted closer to me on the couch, and Juan held up both hands. "I'm sorry. We've bombarded you with too much information at once. We really want you to stay. If you're as powerful as we are hoping, then you will be an asset for the whole warlock and witch community in this upcoming—there I go again. Hitting you with too much at once. We don't need to talk about everything right now. Get a good night's rest and then let Talon show you and your friend around tomorrow. He can answer any questions you might have."

I thought about one of the reasons I wanted to come here tonight. I straightened my spine and held my shoulders back. If they felt that I could possibly deserve to wear a crown, I needed to act like I thought I could, too. Maybe I would get more answers. My gut was saying that Juan was arrogant and needed to prove his worth. That whatever this camp really was it helped boost his ego, and he had no intention of letting anyone take that from him. So why was he shoving this crown off on me? It was time for a wow factor. A round of shock should do that and the only way that I knew how to do that was to show my hand. Well, not all of my cards. Just a few.

"Actually, I had a question right now. Would you know anything about a key?"

Juan glared at me for a few intense seconds before he and Talon shared a look. Juan's frown line on his forehead deepened in thought. "I understood you knew nothing of the supernatural community?"

"That is true. However, a man came into town about the same time as Talon, and he has been giving me a little education on the keys and portals."

Juan's voice was harsh. "Who was this man?"

Tandi had gone deadly still beside me. I wasn't the only one that had picked up on the charged atmosphere, but now we were getting somewhere. Juan's false smile no longer resided on his face.

"His name is Jamison Bradford."

"The Werewolf Prince?" Juan slammed a hand down on his armchair. "Talon, how could you not know this? Were you not following her?"

Following me? And here I thought he was just stalking.

"I actually did know. But I didn't think it was important," Talon said nervously.

"Of course, it's important, you imbecile. This changes everything." Juan stood up to pace the floors. "He wouldn't have allowed her to come here if he knows what she could mean to us, to our cause, and with Jamison's powers and connections, you can believe he knows. This is a trap. She comes in, asking about the key of all things." He pointed a finger at Talon. "And you have led him right to our door."

Juan was so mad he had spittle forming at the corners of his mouth. I grabbed Tandi's hand.

Tandi held my fingers in a crushing grip. "Maybe we should just go," she said, as her voice shook with fear.

I knew it was too late for that. Besides, something was calling me. My eyes darted around the room seeking but not finding.

Juan barked out a laugh. "Oh, that's funny." He strode for the door of the cabin. He called a couple of names in rapid succession and two beefy warlocks walked in. They looked as if they were prepared for anything, with all the ammo they had strapped to their chests. Things were definitely not going well. "They can no longer stay as guests, though. Show them where they will be sleeping while I try to do damage control."

After Juan left, no one said anything for several minutes but with his departure came hope. Not to run. We couldn't do that. Not when we were so close to getting what Jamison needed. I needed. The world needed us to find. The key.

"I think it's best if we just head back home," Tandi said in a hushed voice. "Yeah, I've just remembered that I have a ton of things that I have to do."

Talon's head dropped as he stared at the floor. His auburn hair fell lightly over one of his eyes. No one moved as we watched him come to some sort of decision. "My motto in life is if the ends justify the means then do it, but know that I really wish things didn't have to be like this."

I squeezed Tandi's hand as the warlocks came to stand before us. One of the men blew some kind of powder into our faces, and that was the last thing I remembered before I collapsed onto Tandi.

chapter thirteen

I woke up as one of the warlocks jostled my head as he stepped over a fallen log while carrying me. The other warlock carried a limp Tandi over his shoulder like a sack of potatoes. Without letting the warlock know I was awake, I did my best to scan our surroundings in hopes that if the opportunity of escape should present itself, we would at least know the way out. To the right of me, I saw something slither into the water, and I knew we would not be fleeing by that route. Even if we didn't get eaten by an alligator, there was no way I could swim the distance to the other side of the bank with an unconscious Tandi.

The men's boots clamored along the path as they took us across a rope bridge and headed down a narrow trail. Fifteen minutes later, we finally came upon what looked to be an old hunting camp. It was far enough away from the other shacks to give me hope that we could escape. We entered the small building, which reeked of animal remains. My stomach rolled at the stench.

They dropped us both on the floor of the cabin. It took everything I had not to groan when I hit the hard floor. One warlock nudged my foot. "That was more than enough powder to keep the witch out for the rest of the night, but we still have been ordered to guard the door."

Ha! Guess again, sucker.

The other one grumbled before they both left. I waited for what seemed like hours, but was just mere minutes, before I decide it was safe to move. There were two windows and a door. No bathroom and no electricity. The moon shone bright enough for me to see that Tandi lay unmoving beside me on the floor. I tried to wake her, but it was impossible. What if whatever we inhaled had a different effect on humans? My tears kept falling on her barely rising chest; this was my fault. I shouldn't have brought her here. My gut was telling me there was danger all around us, and yet I let her walk into the swamp with me. For what? The key? So stupid!

My heart was racing. As I rocked Tandi in my arms, I thought about Jamison. Was I bait? I knew that he was hiding something. What if this was it? Get me behind enemy lines but for what? Would he be using me as a distraction as he came for the key? If he was as powerful as Juan claimed, why did he need my help at all? What if he was just using me to isolate the key to create a distraction? If that was the case, then this could be a trap. He marked me, so he could find the key. The key, he had a feeling was right here in this camp. His mark could have nothing to do with my safety. I lay Tandi down as I felt my anger boiling. The last thing I needed was to set Tandi on fire. My gut clenched. No, none of that made sense. My brain was telling me that it was a huge possibility that I had trusted the wrong person but my gut was congratulating me.

I could control the elements. I wasn't totally helpless. The mark on my shoulder itched. Oh, yes. I was totally capable of creating fire right now. I would burn down this whole cabin if it wouldn't betray my secret. I couldn't let these people know I could do more than fog.

After hours of planning, the morning light streamed through the window. There was a knock on my door.

Talon came in with a sheepish smile on his face. "Hey, I'm so sorry that it had to come to this." He made a grand gesture with his arm, looking disgusted with the surroundings. "I really hate that you were pulled into the middle of this. But I promise—" Another knock on the door interrupted him. "Come in."

A witch entered, carrying a long, white wedding dress. Talon's face paled before he said, "Hang it on the windowsill and give us a moment."

"What is that?"

"Juan thinks that we would be a good match. We're both the same age. I am pretty powerful for such a young warlock, and I really do like you." He gave a nervous laugh, and the pit in my stomach grew. "I mean, what's not to like? I wish we had lots of time. Time for me to win you over. Convince you that I'm pretty likable, too. But that's just not the case. Time is always ticking and if Juan is correct, there are people searching for you right now. We just received word that the Undertaker is looking for you. It is never good when Death comes calling. Plus, I'm sure Jamison is searching for you too. He has had this weird vendetta against my family since before I was born. Juan will be able to protect you, though, if you vow to be a part of our community. We can help you escape the Undertaker and the Prince of Wolves."

"Again. What. Is. That!" I yelled, pointing to the white dress.

"The witch community is divided. A true Queen can bring them back together again. You can command them to follow you and because most are loyal, they will. Juan thinks that until we figure out just what you're capable of, you need a king to stand beside you to protect you and to guide you in making the right choices. My uncle will officiate the ceremony tying us together."

Dread hit me. "Is Juan your uncle?"

"Oh, yes, sorry. I thought you knew that."

The same uncle Jamison thought killed his parents? I felt my blood boiling inside me. I crossed my arms to try and contain some of the rage that I'm feeling. There was no way in Hell that I was marrying Talon. I knew this but for whatever crazy reason they did not. I couldn't lose my temper and turn the boy in front of me into a pile of ash for two reasons. One being Tandi and the other was steadily and silently calling to me. The key was close, and it was just a matter of time before I found it.

"I won't be manipulated into whatever game you're playing, and I sure as hell don't want to get married."

"I'm sorry, but Juan will force you to get married."

"Let me rephrase. I will not get married. Period. End of discussion."

"You don't understand. I let you bring your friend here as leverage. My uncle allowed her to come this far into our camp for the same reasoning. She is here to make sure things go smoothly. Try to understand that my uncle always gets what he wants. His reasoning is always to better our community, our goals, our future."

My gut screamed in agony. This boy meant what he said and worse I knew that he had killed before. No matter the image that he was trying to portray, he had blood on his hands and I was willing to bet it was innocent blood.

"You will hurt my friend if I don't agree to marry you?"

He dared to look somber. "I'm afraid so, but I'm sure it won't come to that. Especially once you realize this is your true destiny. Ever since your mother went missing, the witch community has been broken. There has been no order. With you here now—our true queen—we can unite everyone. There will be one law. Your law. Our law. With my uncle helping you to make the right decisions and my power backing you, we can win the war."

"Win the war against who?" Even though I knew his answer, I wanted to hear him say it.

"The Lux. They think they know it all but if they did, they wouldn't have lost the keys to begin with. They are undeserving of the power the keys hold."

"You want to open the portals?"

"If the prisoners of the portals will pledge loyalty to us—to our cause—then yes. I will open the portal."

"You can't control everyone that comes over, though. Why risk it? Why risk your life?"

"My uncle thinks that your mother hid you because you were even more powerful than she was. He thinks you are strong enough to control who comes over."

My gut bypassed my brain taking the lead on this one. I was better off denying the truth -of his words. There were some cards I was willing to play but my potential…

no I couldn't show them that hand. "Sorry. You'd be wrong if you believed that. This key, where is it?"

"Why do you want to know so bad?"

"Call me intrigued. There has been a lot of talk about it."

He gave a shrug. "My uncle has it. I'm sure after we're married, and you have taken your pledge to our community, he will let you see it."

What they didn't know was I wanted this key. Really wanted it. Just like I had really wanted to find Colby. I just needed to stall until I had it in my hands.

"When is this so-called marriage to take place?"

"Tonight." He looked at the still unconscious Tandi. "Your friend won't be able to leave camp. Ever. But she will be safe here. I will try to make both of your lives as pleasant as possible. You just have to give me a shot."

Please. What a creep. Him and his family were crazy. Threating my friend's life... I have never felt so angry. When the moment was right, I would set them on fire like ants. But until then, I would try to act docile. For Tandi's sake, I swallowed my anger.

Talon headed towards the door. "You don't have to wear the dress, but it would please me. I want this day to be special for you. I'll step outside while you dress." Please him? What would please me is if he fell on a knife. I couldn't let my rage out of its cage yet. My gut was telling me to hold off on burning the place to ashes. But he would meet his fate soon, and I would be the one to deliver him to it.

I took a couple of deep breaths before I jerked the dress off of its hanger. I needed Tandi to wake up. I couldn't escape without her.

I quickly took off the outfit I was wearing and shimmied my way into the tight-fitting, mermaid-style wedding dress. I somehow managed to get the stupid thing zipped, and it took everything I had not to vomit all over the glistening white ivory.

There was a knock before Talon entered, holding a box and wearing a huge smile. "You are so beautiful." I'd been locked in a dirty cabin, so I was sure 'beautiful' was an overstatement at this point. I felt grimy and tired, but I was ready. Ready for whatever lay ahead of me. He opened the box and pulled out a beautiful crown. It had many different sized points growing out of the base, encrusted with diamonds. The points resembled icicles. "It took us a while to hunt this down. My uncle had to pull a lot of strings, but it was worth it for the look on your face. It is said your grandmother made this crown out of ice that will never melt."

He walked over to me and placed it on my head. "We need you to look like the queen that everyone will fear one day."

"What if I choose to rule with love instead of fear?"

He wrinkled his nose. "We believe a strong hand wields the best crops. Now, we should go. Everyone is waiting for us outside the main gym. After the ceremony, I'll show you around the compound." I felt my anger bubbling out. No, I couldn't ruin the plan now. Whatever the hell the plan was. Besides at that very moment, I felt it. The key. It was here, and it was close by. I could be docile for a little while longer. My mark tingled. Here is to hoping that Jamison knows that I might be in over my head.

I laid a hand on his arm. "Please, Talon, don't force this. I'm begging you."

His knuckles tilted my chin up. His touch was revolting, but I did my best not to flinch. "I will become king today, and we will rule together. This is fate."

That's what he thought. Guess again, buddy. Another warlock walked into the already cramped space. He laid a hand on Tandi.

"Get the hell away from her," I shouted.

Talon placed a hand on my arm. "It's okay. He is healing her, so the drugs will wear off faster. I thought you would want your best friend there with you. I was trying to be accommodating."

"You were the one that had her drugged in the first place!" Docile. I was supposed to remain docile. A couple of deep breaths in and out. "Yes, I would like her there."

Tandi started stirring. She moaned as she tried to sit up. "Ugh. Am I dead? Do me a favor. Don't play funeral music, but put on some Lynyrd Skynyrd, offer shots of Tequila... Patrón, because I wouldn't settle for anything less, and for the love of Pete, no open casket. Make sure to use a headshot of me that is fabulous and no carnations. I hate those damn flowers."

I ran over to her, kneeling by her side. My dress ripped, and I took great satisfaction in that sound. The pretty dress looked ratchet now, huh? I gave her a warm hug. "I was so worried about you!" Turning to Talon, I asked,

"Can you give us a moment alone? I would like to catch her up on everything."

He hesitated for a moment. "There are a lot of witches in this compound. You would be stupid to try anything." I quieted my rage and nodded my head instead in understanding.

"I'll be right outside."

After I told her everything that happened, she said, "I'm assuming you have a plan? Light this whole mother on fire if you have to, but we have to do something. These people are crazy."

A smile lit my face. "I agree. I was just waiting for you to wake up." I extended a hand to her. "Shall we?"

With Tandi by my side, we left the cabin hand in hand. There was a good chance I wouldn't be able to control any of my powers, but it was a risk we were willing to take. I also knew where the coveted key was. I could feel it like a beacon. Calling me. And we were headed right to it.

chapter fourteen

My dress caught on every fallen branch and leaf on the ground. Much to Talon's dismay, at one point I stopped and ripped the material, so it hit above my kneecaps. It was still not the perfect escape outfit, but it would be easier to run this way once I found the opportunity to make a break for it. But first, I had to say hello to the key. Like a dog with a bone, I wasn't giving it up. Tandi noticed my sneakers and snorted but made no snide commentary. I kind of pictured my wedding day differently, too. My heartbeat was racing and by this point my mark was thrumming with energy. We finally made it to the facility where I was told everyone ate and trained.

"Well, Jiminy freakin' Cricket. Did any of these people RSVP? Will we have enough food?" Tandi mock whispered.

A corner of my lip lifted. She had total faith I would be able to get us out of this mess we were in. My mark began to itch again. I ignored it. I had too many things on my plate to be worrying about that right now. Jamison would either know I was in trouble or he wouldn't. Either way, I couldn't rely on him to save me and my best friend. I needed to trust my gut and save us.

I whispered, "When you see the fog, run. Run as fast as your legs will carry you. Not sure if I can control myself. Try to make it to the car."

She gave me a tight nod and my chest constricted. I would get us out of this.

My wedding site looked like something out of Deliverance. The lot was recently cleared of trees, and the fresh dirt was nothing but mud due to the recent rain. There was a small cement building that couldn't have passed inspection code if they wanted it to. It haphazardly leaned to the left. Two big bins of trash overflowed on either side of the building. To the right of the building stood Juan—and the key. All of my energy was entirely focused on him. Yes, without a shadow of a doubt Juan had the key. He was looking all smug in a black ceremonial robe that probably matched his heart. Ah, and there it was. The key was under the robe. Good to know. I would take it from his corpse. Talon went to stand by his uncle, where they began a whispered conversation. Then they both turned to face a large group of about seventy-five or so witches and warlocks standing with their backs to the swamp. I was going to let my gut decide how this should play out. This was my fate.

I adjusted the crown on my head that my grandmother had worn and my mother refused to claim. Was I claiming it? It was obvious these people should have another option for a leader, but were they firmly in the Degenerates' camp, or were they just lost souls? Maybe I should give them a choice before I flaunt my flaw—no, my gift—to the best of my ability. This was it. I was about to either make history or fail miserably, but either way, I would give it a hundred percent. I left Tandi at the outer edge of the semi-circle and went to stand between Juan, Talon, and the witches.

Addressing the witches, I asked, "Are there any of you that would willingly follow me… your queen without this union taking place?"

Some looked to the ground. Some shook their heads, and the ones I disliked the most laughed. All righty then. That answered my question. They were team Juan all the way. Might as well go ahead and start the show. Fog swirled around Tandi, separating her from Talon and Juan. I saw my friend's blond hair swinging wildly about her as she took off at a dead run through the forest. I sent up a silent prayer that she would remain safe.

I recalled Jamison's kiss, how it burned my insides, and left me feeling like a drug addict wanting more. The wind stirred with my memory. Soon, I was able to replace the image of Jamison's kiss with what I wanted—the wind to blow like an isolated category five hurricane. And it did. Trees were uprooted, and everyone that had been standing in front of me was thrown backwards into the waist-deep, murky water. Someone—Talon—was shouting my name as I made it to the bank of the swamp, unfazed by the wind. Witches screamed, trying to crawl over one another to exit the water, but the wind wasn't on their side.

I reached a hand into the water, my parents' images flashing through my mind. The water turned to a solid sheet of ice, trapping the witches and warlocks in a frozen cage. Would they freeze to death? I didn't have a clue, but at least this way they couldn't stab me in the back while I dealt with the crazy family duo. I walked back through the fog towards a confused Talon and an irate Juan.

"Hey, boys."

"Quick," Juan said, "Take care of her."

Juan brought out the key and ran towards a piece of shimmering air right between two old moss-covered trees. His back was to me, but I knew what he was doing. He was opening a portal. I could feel the magic in the air.

Talon took a step towards me, and I placed a hand on his chest. "Talon, please stop him. If he opens that portal, we could all die."

"I'm sorry. We can't let a power like yours go unchecked." That's cute that he thought he was a match for me. Ever. "If only you would have joined us." He brought out a silver blade, pressing it against my throat. Then he froze. I was mad. Mad that he was making me choose my life over his. With my hand still on his chest, I iced the blood in his veins. His lips turned blue, crystals coating his eyelashes. Within seconds, he was frozen solid.

Juan closed the portal, but not before ten supernaturals came over. I'd been wondering what demons looked like. I wished I were still wondering. All of them were more than six feet tall of pure muscle and wide as linebackers with skin red as blood. Each one of them had a set of black horns sprouting from their heads that varied in length. Black onyx eyes took in their surroundings before they spoke in a tongue I'd never heard before. Fear gripped me. Did ice work on demons? Fire?

It took them less than thirty seconds to understand that someone allowed them to come here. Juan was smirking until one of the demons said something in a foreign language, pointing at the key. Two of the demons broke off and headed towards Juan. Their intent was clear. They wanted what allowed them out of their cage. Juan's survival skills must have kicked in because he took off at a dead run through the forest.

Maybe I should run, too. My gut told me I had every right to be scared of these creatures. My eyes flickered side to side, scanning the woods. That's when I noticed Jamison sprinting through the woods. I was so happy to see him I could have broken out in a dance while screaming his name but I would have to save my non-rhythmic dancing skills for later. The demons didn't seem to notice him… yet. Jamison's eyes never left the eight demons who started to fan out around me. I spread my fog to the right of me, giving Jamison as much coverage as I could. He might be the only secret weapon I could use at this point.

Two demons crept in on me, whispering to each other. With my left hand, I called the wind to me, and it came as easy and natural as breathing. My wind didn't knock them back like it did the witches, but they didn't come closer, either. Once I was safe and survived this, I would congratulate myself on calling wind and creating fog at the same time.

Jamison emerged from the mist, taking the demon he was now directly in front of by surprise. He had a long blade in his hand resembling a machete. The blade gleamed as it made an arc in the air. My wind faltered as the demon's head rolled off his shoulders and hit the ground. I chastised myself. Now wasn't the time to get squeamish. My queasiness cost me a precious foot of distance. The two demons on my left gained ground towards me. Jamison was a blur as he moved in and out of demons. Without looking, I could now identify the sound that came with decapitation. I swallowed the bile rising. Not now! Get sick later.

Jamison had made a semi-circle and was now behind the two demons on my left that I was still keeping at bay with my wind. Both demons heard his approach and turned on him to attack in a concentrated effort. Jamison would be fine. He was big and strong but my moment of concern cost me dearly. A demon had crept up on my right side without me knowing it and in any second he would have me in his grip. I threw my right hand out at him and smiled as fire consumed him. Hot waves coated his skin as he rode a bed of fiery waves. He tilted his head back, roaring with laughter. Of course, fire wouldn't hurt him. He was probably born of fire. I changed my tactics and prayed my mistake wasn't a deadly one. Without looking, I knew Jamison had taken care of the two demons on my left and was engaged with another. The demon grabbed me with one beefy hand, and I swung my left hand at him, hoping the wind would phase him. He twisted my right arm until I heard it snap, not only was it broken, but the ligaments were torn. Tears filled my eyes. Ice shot through me, mingling with wind. The demon holding me turned to a solid piece of ice, and I kicked him, shattering him into a million pieces. All the king's horses and all the king's men couldn't put him back together again.

My knees crumbled under me as I cradled my arm. Two demons emerged from the woods, dragging a bloody

Juan between them. One demon tossed the key up in the air. They stopped when they saw their comrades scattered all over the woods without their heads. One demon spat a command, and the other demon holding the key took off running back through the woods.

The last standing demon dropped Juan onto the ground as he slowly walked towards Jamison. He had to know that he couldn't beat the boy who just single-handedly took out seven of his friends, but maybe that wasn't the point of this fight. Maybe he was cannon fodder. Which didn't make sense. I would think that the Degenerates weren't a self-sacrificing lot. Then again, maybe this demon was just stupid enough to think that he could take down Jamison. The demon danced around Jamison, never letting him get too close. I got tired of the game he was playing and stumbled to my feet. The pain in my arm was enough to make me want to black out. But not yet. With my good arm, I made a tunnel of fog around the demon, temporarily blinding him. The familiar sound of Jamison's blade came again. As my adrenaline wore off, I found myself back on the ground before the demon's head rolled towards me.

Jamison knelt next to me. "How badly are you hurt?"

"Pretty freaking bad."

"I can help, but it will hurt."

He took my injured arm in his hands and closed his eyes. His long eyelashes cast a shadow over his perfect cheeks as he concentrated. Unbearable pain radiated from me as I felt my tendons knitting back together and the bone snapping back into place. Sweat beaded my upper lip, and I felt like I was going to faint. My head dropped

to his shoulder as tears trailed down my face. The pain started to fade into a dull ache. After a few minutes, there was no pain at all.

"The key! You have to go get it. If you hurry maybe you can—"

"No, it's too late. Besides Ariana might have gave me a heads up."

My eyes narrowed. "About?"

"She told me not to leave you. So here I am."

I frowned up at him as I flexed my fingers and bent my arm. It was healed. "How did you do that?"

"I can heal others if I agree to take their pain. Another benefit Ariana bestowed upon me and my brother."

"Are you in pain right now?"

I noticed his right arm hung limply by his side. "I heal so quickly that the pain has already begun to fade." With his good arm, he tucked my hair behind my ear. "You did really well tonight."

"How did you know where to find me? The mark?" Then I thought of what Juan had said earlier. Was this all this a set up to find the key? But why would he have taken the time to heal me instead of letting the demon escape with the key?

"Yeah, it let me know that you were in trouble. You probably felt it tingling, so I knew that—"

"Help," Juan moaned.

A cloud of emotions passed over Jamison's face as he stood. He walked over to Juan and jerked him up by his shirt.

"Hey, Juan, how's it going?" He poked a finger into a cut on Juan's arm, making the older man hiss. "Hmm, not so good I see. So, there has been a rumor going around that you were behind the attack on my parents. Is that true?"

Juan's brown eyes were frazzled. "No! Of course not. I would have never hurt the queen or king."

My gut tightened. "He's lying," I said.

Jamison never took his eyes off of Juan. "Yes, he is."

Juan shouted, "Don't let him kill me. I can tell you about your family, help you to understand your powers, and your—"

Jamison punched Juan so hard through the chest I heard the rib cage breaking. I averted my eyes when his hand came out with a bloody heart.

Jamison mumbled, "That was too good of a death for you." Blood covered his hands, and he took a moment to clean them off on Talon's frozen form. Apparently, I was the only one who was squeamish. "We need to get out of here."

I had one question burning inside of me. But did I want the answer? Gathering my courage, I asked, "Did you use me as bait? So you could have your revenge?"

His answer was simple. "No."

"You didn't mark me, so you could find your enemy?"

"No. I marked you so I could find you if you needed me."

Truth and truth.

"You could have ignored Ariana and gone after the key, but you chose to stay."

"I'll always choose you, Charlie."

"Even if it means the world will come to an end?" I asked.

"Without you, I could not care less if the end was now."

Then he kissed me tenderly. When he pulled back his eyes shone with something more than just lust. He looked at me as if I was the most priceless object in the world. Most people hope that they can find that one person that just gets them. That makes them smile at the end of a long day or cheers them on when they feel as if they can't take one more step in this race that we call life. He was looking at me like I was his person. Like I belonged to him.

A loud sound crashed through the underbrush. What now? A moment later, Tandi appeared, driving an ATV.

"It took me forever to find the keys to this thing." She noticed Jamison standing beside me. "Oh, hey, hotness. Hop on, you two lovebirds. I've got places to be." She assessed the damage around her. The sea of witches frozen in the water, the decapitated demons, and the dead Juan before she noticed the frozen statue of Talon. "Y'all have been busy. Sucks that Face had to die but let's be honest, he would have been a terrible husband."

Jamison's eyebrows rose. "Ah, now I get the wedding dress." I looked down at the torn, filthy dress. "Nice tennis shoes, though." He walked over to the ice sculpture known as Talon and with a swift kick to the center of the ice block Talon burst into millions of pieces.

"Was that necessary?" I asked.

Jamison stood there with his fist clenched looking like a dangerous angel that was on the verge of losing his temper. "He tried to take something that matters to me." Then he looked at me. For the first time his cocky arrogant self was replaced with something else. In that moment, he looked vulnerable and something in me broke. "You don't belong to him."

I didn't know how to handle this Jamison but I knew that I wanted… no, I needed to reassure him. "Of course I don't."

He gave me a nod. His sexy smile returned while he steered us around the ice. "We need to get out of here."

And just like that Jamison's swag returned in full force. I wanted to roll my eyes, but I was trying not to step on any squishy limbs as I headed to the ATV.

$\mathcal{A}$s we made our way to our cars, Tandi received a phone call. She needed to get home and quick. Her mother had brought her close to tears with her belittling. Tandi's mother was a horrible woman whose sole reason for having a child was because it was what was expected. A box had been checked at Tandi's birth, so the next task was to make Tandi's life miserable with her own expectations. And what was expected of Tandi right now was to come home and put on a show. The mayor was coming over to their house, and her mother needed Tandi to pretend they were a loving family. Tandi wasn't a people pleaser except for when it came to her parents. She had always wanted what they hadn't been able to give her. Unconditional love. I gathered her up in my arms and gave her a hug so fierce I was scared I would crush her. She groaned about her ribs before I let her go. She gave us a wave as she jumped into my car. She was going to drive my car, and I would ride back with Jamison.

The drive back to my house started out as a quiet one. I was so disappointed we lost the key. I wanted to help Jamison save the world, and we were so close just to come up empty-handed. Juan had opened the door for maybe twenty seconds, and ten demons had escaped. Now that I had seen what an open portal could do, I was more determined to find that key again.

We were an hour into our trip back home when I broke the silence. "What's the plan now?" I asked.

"I find the demon with the key."

"No. We find the key. I feel connected to it now. I know I could help."

His grip tightened on the steering wheel as he looked over at me. "Demons are a tougher crowd than witches."

"I'm not an average witch."

"That's true. If you're sure you want to hunt down the key, then we will head out tonight. Oh and Charlie?"

"Hmm?"

He gave me a once over that made my mouth dry. "I like the crown."

I had a smile on my face for the next hour as I contemplated calling my brother. We would be home soon and I really should call him, but what I needed to say to him couldn't be done over the phone. Maybe I could ask him to come home early. My brother might become angry with me for not telling him sooner, but one thing was for certain, he would never stop loving me. Then again, why did I need to drag him into all of this? My head hit the back of the headrest a couple of times in frustration. I really shouldn't go traipsing after a demon without talking to him first. What if something happened to me?

"Are you going to tell me what's on your mind, or are you just going to keep banging your head while dramatically sighing?"

"Would you mind if we left in the morning? I need to talk to my brother."

Jamison shook his head. "I don't think that's a good idea," he said, as he parked the car into our oyster-shell driveway. "What can he possibly do for you other than worry? And we really do need to be going. Grab some clothes and maybe a snack bag and we'll head out."

My gut tightened. Red flag. He was hiding something. We both got out of the car and headed inside. My mind was working overtime. "I'm just going to take a quick shower. Wipe the mud off of me." I ran upstairs and tossed the crown onto my bed. I headed to the bathroom and took the quickest shower of my life. As soon as I was done I left the water running so that Jamison would think that I was still in the shower. I ditched my clothes for jeans and a tank top. I was buttoning my jeans as I dialed my brother.

"Hey, sis. Everything okay?"

"No, actually it's not. Can you come home?"

"What is—"

"Hello? Wes?" The line was dead. I was cradling the phone with dread when Jamison walked into my room. Did he cut the phone line?

"Werewolf hearing, remember?" He took the phone out of my hand and put it back on the receiver. "I really wish you wouldn't have done that."

Confusion hit me hard. There was no way I could have been so wrong about him. I knew instinctively that I had

nothing to fear from Jamison. He would never hurt me so anger colored my words. "Why do you not want me talking to my brother?" I stood immobile as Jamison went to the window and pulled back the curtain, as if he was looking for someone.

He tilted his head back and sighed. "And so it begins."

"What?"

There was a crash downstairs that had Jamison speeding out of my bedroom. I trailed after him as he literally jumped down the steps and ran for the living room. Before I could follow, some force knocked me back into my room. The door slowly closed and the lock clicked into place.

The smell of peat smoke filled my room. It was strong, almost overwhelming and comforting all at the same time. A swirl of thick smoke appeared in my bedroom carrying a man dressed in all black. He was tall and wiry with a face many girls had fallen for. Jamison had a face of an angel, just as this boy had the face of something of equal magnitude but darker. I was staring into the face of the Undertaker, and he didn't look happy at all.

"Tell me that you're not the infamous Undertaker?"

My brother's amber eyes looked contrite. "What gave it away, the scythe or the all-black attire? All kidding aside, I'm sorry you had to find out like this." He held up a finger, silencing me. "Tell me quickly… the wolf that is currently coming up the stairs enemy or friend?"

"Friend." I thought. "You weren't off selling paintings, were you?"

"I actually do have an art gallery in New York, and my paintings have been making me a handsome commission, but that's not the reason I've been away."

"What have you been doing?"

"It's complicated."

Jamison broke down my door with one swift kick. He didn't stop moving until he was directly in between Wes and me.

Wes looked at the splintered door frame then at Jamison. "A little on edge, are we?"

I stepped from behind Jamison. "What is your deal, Jamison? And don't act like you didn't know who my brother was. You knew all along, didn't you? Is that why you didn't want me calling him?"

We were completely ignoring Wes as we glared at each other. Or maybe I was doing the glaring.

"Yes." Jamison crossed his arms over his chest. "At first I didn't tell you about your brother because I thought he was the one who had the key. Then when Talon came into the picture I realized I was mistaken. Then I didn't tell you about your brother because I thought finding out about him being the Undertaker and a Degenerate might be a hard pill to swallow."

Wes shrugged. "He has a point. Though I would like to take this time to point out that I'm not a Degenerate. Not that anyone is listening to me, anyways."

I drove my index finger into Jamison's chest. "And after you realized that it was Juan that held the key? Why didn't you tell me then?"

Jamison was completely silent for several seconds. "I didn't want to be the one to tell you about your brother."

"I'm the grim reaper, not dying of a disease. Jeez!"

I was outraged. Both of these boys were a part of my life. And both of them had kept a secret from me. One that was huge. I was pissed and struggling to hide my emotions when, my brother said, "And you, little sister? You smell like power. When were you going to tell me that you came into your powers?"

"Probably around the same time that you were going to explain to me that I had them."

Wes's smile grew on his handsome face. "Touché little sister. I've royally screwed up."

Some of the anger left me. I've always struggled staying mad at my brother. "I didn't want to burden you with my problems when you were off trying to sell your paintings."

His smile dropped. "I hate that you ever felt like you couldn't come to me. I'm sorry on many different levels."

"When I found out about all of this, I honestly thought that our dad was human and you took after him. I thought all of this would freak you out." That was the understatement of the year. "How am I a witch, and you're an Undertaker?"

"First, you're Queen of the Warlocks and Witches. And I am the Undertaker because that is what our father was."

I needed to sit for this. I found myself walking towards the bed. I picked up the crown and studied the ice-encrusted diamonds at the base of the circle as I tried to picture our sweet, shy, and humble dad as the Undertaker. The one that tucked me into bed every night and kissed every boo-boo. No way. "Are you sure?"

"Positive. The Underworld talks. Apparently, Mom fell in love with the bad boy of the other side. Our dad. Her father, the King of Warlocks, was happy over the union, but right after they were married, our grandfather was murdered by his own brother. Mom ran away when she found out she was pregnant with me. She didn't want us to be hunted down like her father was, and she was unsure of who to trust. She put a spell over this whole town, so no one could find us. Then some idiot at a gas station decided to rob the place. She got in the way, and a bullet killed her instantly. One of the most powerful witches to ever live and she was killed by a human. Once she died, the spell was lifted."

Tears streamed down my cheeks. "And Dad?"

"Dad was shot, too, but a bullet couldn't kill him." He gathered me in his arms. "There is life after this, Charlie. Dad wanted to be with her, and I don't blame him. He made the decision right then to turn over his soul. To willingly die. The moment he passed was the moment I became the Undertaker. I've been trying to learn the ropes ever since."

"Is that what you were off doing?"

"No, that's the part that's complicated."

"Give me the short version and try your best to un-complicate it."

"The man Merek, that killed his own brother, our grandfather, recently died at the hands of the Werewolf

King." He nodded towards Jamison. "The prince's brother. Merek has a son, Cecil, that is currently on a mission to hunt down the rest of the keys to destroy the Lux. Not to mention, owning the keys is very profitable and powerful. Cecil can't go against the strongest of the Lux without help, so he found a girl by the name of Tamara, who wears two crowns. She's rumored to be a very powerful vampire princess, and she's also a zombie queen. Basically, her mother is the ruler of the undead, leaving her daughter a legacy, and Tamara, thanks to her father, can control the dead. It's an occupational hazard for me. A conflict of interest, if you will. Cecil plans on marrying her because she comes with her own army, outnumbering the Lux and Degenerates put together."

"So Cecil thinks if he marries this girl, then he can go around collecting all the keys because his wife has an army of vampires backing her, plus she can raise the dead?"

"As long as there is death, I will live. Once I harvest a soul, their power becomes mine. If Tamara raises the dead, I relinquish that power back to its original owner. This girl could actually be the death of me."

Jamison, who had been quiet during all of this, said, "We have to go. A demon that escaped got a good look at your sister. He probably has her scent. We need to get far away from here."

There was a knock on our front door. My heart started racing, which was crazy. A demon, even a polite one, wouldn't just ring the doorbell.

Jamison and Wes both said at the same time, "Tandi."

I ran downstairs to get the door. On my way, I thought about how Tandi was going to flip when she found out who her very first crush was. I was still angry that my brother didn't sit down at some point and tell me about our parents, himself, and what I should expect, but as a child who had lost her parents suddenly, I decided I wasn't going to hold a grudge. He was my brother, and the only one I had.

chapter sixteen

I opened the door to see Tandi in a beautiful, black sequined gown.

"I thought you were eating dinner with your family and the mayor?"

She shoved in past me. "That was before he decided to get sloshed and make grabby hands at me. I'm sure my mom will notice I'm missing soon. Or not. She was pretty wasted, too. I figured Scooby and the gang needed me to help find the key anyways."

Wes came into the living room. "Tandi knows about us? About the key?"

I rolled my eyes. Really? Like I would have kept anything from her. A stupid question deserved no answer. I shut the door and followed Tandi to the couch. "Oh, and get this. My brother is the Undertaker."

"No shit. Hmm." She eyed him up and down. "I can see that. He's always had that bad boy swagger going on." Tandi narrowed her eyes at him. "You couldn't put Jenny on your list, could you?"

"Sorry, no." Wes was trying hard not to smile. "It doesn't work like that."

Her bottom lip stuck out in a fake pout. I laughed as I patted her on the arm. "Pity, I know. So before you came, Jamison was saying the demons might have got my scent and could show up. This might not be the safest place for you."

"Well, neither is the mayor's lap. I'll just go with you guys. Think of me as the mascot."

Wes sat in one of the wingback chairs. "Oh, witches will definitely show up. Not sure about demons, though. My soothsayer didn't mention them. She also told me not to rush home until I received a phone call from Charlie."

Jamison narrowed his eyes. "You have a soothsayer?"

"Not that it's any of your business, but yes. Ever since I came into my powers, she's been there for me to assure me I wasn't losing my mind. She's also sending me after a key."

Tandi huffed. "Apparently, Jamison, having a soothsayer is all the rage nowadays. They're like freaking iPhones. Everybody has one. Maybe that's what I should ask for, for Christmas. My own back pocket psychic. I wonder if she's better than Siri?"

Jamison studied Wes. "Her name? The soothsayer, what's her name?"

"Why would I tell you that?"

Jamison's eyes started to swirl that familiar honey color. That's all we needed.

"Wes! Please?" I begged.

"Fine." Wes sighed. "Her name is Ariana."

No freakin' way. I looked at Wes in confusion and asked no one in particular, "So, the Ariana who basically raised Jamison and his brother since they were little is the same Ariana who reached out to you recently? The same soothsayer who had Jamison come here to collect the key also wants you to collect a key? But not the same key?"

"It can't be the same key," Jamison said.

"According to Ariana, my key will come after I find Tamara. She gave me some cryptic message about love being the only thing more powerful than death."

Jamison sighed. "Yep, that's definitely Ariana." His eyes cut to me briefly before he ran a hand through his tousled hair. "She told me to keep my eye on the prize and I won't lose."

Jamison's body stiffened, his eyes turning to honey. Wait. I thought we had squashed the friction between the boys. He couldn't possibly be that jealous that Wes had the same soothsayer. Wes stood, pulling a scythe out from thin air.

"What's going on, guys?" I asked.

The walls started to tremble. And the china cabinet in the dining room rattled. Earthquake in Louisiana? No way.

"Freakin' unbelievable," Wes shouted over the rumbling. "They have a sorcerer with them."

"Yep," Jamison said.

"A what?" I squealed.

Jamison grabbed me by the hand, jerking my body to his. "A very powerful wizard who deals in black magic."

"Well, that's just great," Tandi said, as she came to stand next to me. "Can we beat him?"

Both men looked at Tandi like she had just insulted them.

"Of course, we'll beat him," Wes said. "The more powerful they are when they cross over, the better for me."

"We need to get Tandi away from here," I said.

Jamison gave me a concerned look. "You are just as mortal as she is. But, regardless, there is no time now."

The pictures on the walls were falling to the floor. Every shatter made me wince. "Does he plan on taking the whole house down?"

Jamison yelled over the booming sound, "Not if we leave it. Everybody, out the back door."

We all ran out the back of the house and reached the backyard, only to find ourselves swallowed up by a surge of black smoke. Tandi fell to her knees, coughing. Jamison helped her back to her feet, then all hell broke loose. Supernaturals surrounded us.

Wes swirled his scythe in a circle, causing the audience in front of him to show a momentary look of fear. My egotistical brother tilted his head back with laughter.

He said over his shoulder, "Hey, wolf boy, try and keep up. If you can." Then he started fighting the witches one by one, deflecting their blows with his scythe.

"It's funny how they call you the Reaper, but my count will be higher than yours by the end of the night." Jamison looked at Tandi and me. "Ladies, prepare to be amazed."

Then he took off at a dead run, missing my eye roll as he jumped in the air, breaking someone's spine as he went. With a speed that outmatched the opponents on the battlefield, Jamison took his enemies down before they knew what was happening. I called my ice to me with just a thought. It was getting easier. Call me competitive. I aimed to not only keep up with the boys but surpass them.

With that thought, I went to work. Tandi my biggest fan stood beside me oohing and aahing over my victories. She started clapping as I sent icy daggers towards every witch in striking distance. I didn't bother wasting my fire on the demons because my flames were no match for them. Instead, I used wind to keep them at bay. Then I created fog. It slowly crept up to the right of Jamison. Trapping the demon in its clutches, momentarily blinding him so that Jamison could have the element of surprise. It worked so well that I continued to do it for him and my brother. Each time, I got a bellow of thanks. I wondered if I would get credit for assisting? I sent balls of fire towards short and stout creatures I was very unfamiliar with. All of them had a greenish hue to their skin and were covered in warts. Fire seemed to hurt them.

I was sending a blade of ice through a witch who was trying to take out Wes from behind when Tandi shouted, "Fireball! Corner pocket."

I shot flame at the short creature charging towards us. "I'm totally slaying this whole witch thing."

Tandi clapped. "Yassss girl. I am so jelly right now."

A huge demon threw a blade towards us. Tandi screamed as I stopped the blade in mid-air with a wall of air. It clamored to the ground. Jamison had morphed into his wolf form. Jumping over a small creature, he punched the demon through his back, coming away with the demon's heart.

Tandi squeezed onto my arm like I was a hickory tree to her ivy. I resumed picking between ice or fire. With every blade of ice or ball of fire I made, my confidence grew.

Jamison threw a creature at least ten feet into the air, but before gravity kicked in, Wes flung his scythe like a boomerang, decapitating the witch before she hit the ground. Both boys argued over who got the kill. Ugh. Men.

Tandi shook her head. "Both of them are so much alike. They're both angels of death. Well, technically, Wes is just Death, but you get my point."

I did but I couldn't reply. I was too busy keeping her alive. A witch sent a massive fireball towards us, and I redirected it, sending it right back to her.

"Have you noticed their balls look different than yours?" She snorted. "That sounds so naughty, and I didn't even plan that. It just came right out of my mouth."

Wes shouted over the commotion, "Charlie has more power in her balls." He sighed dramatically at Tandi's hysterical laughter. She almost couldn't breathe at this point. "How are you doing over there, wolf boy?"

Jamison grunted as he broke the horns off a demon. "Never better. And you?"

"Peachy."

Ignoring them, I continued to fight right until I felt a familiar tug. The key. It was here. Why in the world would they bring it with them? Regardless it was here, and I needed to find it. I was having a hard time telling most of the demons apart. Every once in a while, one would be taller or wider, but for the most part, they looked exactly alike. But there was no doubt the demon who escaped the swamp with the key was here. I felt it calling me. There were maybe ten Degenerates left. I looked around the bloody battlefield and saw two demons making their way towards me. I let them come.

"Wind?" Tandi suggested. "Ice? Um, you do realize they are getting closer, right?"

"I want them to. They have something I want."

"Yeah, well, there isn't anything in life I want that bad."

I threw a blade of ice at the one on the left. His skin was too thick for the blade to pierce his heart, but it slowed him down. I formed a barrier of wind between him and the other demon, herding him away from his friend. Jamison appeared behind the demon I had stabbed with my ice. He raised his eyebrow in question. I gave him a nod. He could take care of that demon. I had bigger fish to fry. The other demon—the one I really wanted—stalked closer. He was bare-chested, wearing nothing but loose cotton pants. In the front pocket was a bulge I hoped was the key and not his demon goodies. I slammed a blade of ice in him, but someone had been paying attention. Dodging at the last second, the blade hit him in the right shoulder.

He was on me before I could produce another blade. I might have been a little overconfident. Grabbing me by my hair, he tossed me in the air. I landed with the wind knocked out of me, figuratively speaking. Lying on the ground, I used wind to push Tandi out of his reach. Creating a blind spot, I isolated his head with fog, throwing blade after blade of ice until he dropped to his knees. Coming up behind him, I hit him with a hard gust of air, making him topple over. When he hit the ground, the icy swords that were protruding through him went all the way through his tough skin and through his chest. Yes. I wasted no time digging through his pocket.

165

My smile was so huge it almost hurt my face. I held the freaking key—the one that could save the earth in my itty-bitty hand. Hooyah! Clapping came from the right. I looked over my shoulder to see the battle was over, and both Jamison and Wes had been watching me take the demon down.

"You did good, sister."

"Good?" Jamison scoffed. "She beat your count."

Wes shook his head. "No. That's impossible and you're biased, wolf boy, so your opinion doesn't matter."

I walked towards them with my new shiny object when a blast of heat hit me so hard it sent me flying backwards. I checked to make sure nothing was broken when a shadow loomed over me. I looked up at the sky, where a man flew in small circles above us. His black hair was greasy and hung way past his jaw. His hawk-like eyes, crooked nose, and bony frame made him resemble a raven. He smiled at me like I imagined Jack the Ripper smiled at his victims right before they became his prey. This must be the sorcerer they'd mentioned.

My gut told me this was flight time. I really should tell the boys they could take on the birdman by themselves to add another notch in their belt. I wouldn't argue. Nope. In fact, I insisted. I'd done my part. This was where I tapped out. Besides, I was kind of parched anyways. I looked around to see where Jamison and Wes were. They were both trying to get to me, but it seemed like there was some kind of force separating us. I could see Jamison pounding on thin air while yelling my name. Wes seemed to be walking some sort of a perimeter, trying to find a way to get to me. I glanced behind me, and there stood

Tandi in the doorway of our house, beating her palms on nothing. Something was containing me, as if I were in a fishbowl—or worse, a fish in a barrel. I was no lip reader, but I recognized my name and a few choice words flowing from Tandi's mouth. I was in some kind of bubble, just me and the flying freak in the sky. When I thought it couldn't get any worse, I realized I had dropped the key. It was four feet in front of me. I threw an icy blade towards the raven, but he dodged it so easily it might as well have been in slow motion. Great, I was obviously the amateur.

The bird-like man above me made a gesture with his hand, and the ground around me started to quake. The cracks in the ground grew wider and deeper until I was running out of standing room. I tried to figure out my next move as the cracks grew into a huge crevice. Then I was falling. My hands grappled onto anything I could.

Clunks of dirt and rocks came away between my fingers, and I had lost sight of the key. I grabbed hold of a large root in the ground, saving me from free falling into a huge pit of fire the sorcerer had created. I attempted to pull myself out of the hole using the root of the tree, but I kept slipping, and the stupid loop of my jeans was caught on something. With every pull on the root, I heard the fabric tearing on something below me.

My wind could carry me out of the crater. But where would it carry me to? There was no safe ground inside of this bubble. Holding on for dear life, I saw Jamison at the top of the tree. Below me, there was a small cliff. It was barely above the fire, but if I could swing my body, I might be able to land on it. Then again, I might just tumble into the pit. I was running out of options.

chapter seventeen

The distance was too great for Wes to throw his Scythe. Though it didn't stop him from trying. The raven was so invested in what Wes was doing that he didn't notice Jamison who sprang from one of the branches, jumping over the bubble. His body collided with the raven, sending both of them spiraling to the ground on the outer edge of the bubble. The air shifted, and I knew instinctively that whatever trap I was in had vanished. Jamison jerked the sorcerer off the ground, swinging him into the pit. I watched his descent until the fire swallowed him whole, and with his death, the fire started to dissipate; the ground stopped quaking.

Jamison dropped to his stomach along the edge of the huge crater taking up most of our backyard. "Give me your hand."

Using my wind to buoy me up, I took Jamison's hand and let him pull me up beside him.

My eyes clenched shut at what we had just lost… again. "The key. Is it gone?"

"Don't worry about the key. You're safe, and that is all that matters."

My head dropped to his chest. "I feel like it's my fault we keep losing the key."

"That's ridiculous." He stroked my hair for a few minutes. "Ariana told me to never take my eyes off the prize and I didn't. You are far more valuable to me than the key, but we will get it back."

"But how? It was swallowed up in the flames."

"The key is indestructible," Wes said as he came over to stand next to us.

Tandi ran around the edges of the hole and skidded to a stop in front of us. "I thought you were going to be roasted there for a minute."

"Is the sorcerer dead?" I asked.

Jamison nodded. "Yes, and I'm assuming by the glazed look on your brother's face, he reaped the benefits."

Wes held out his arms, watching something we couldn't see. "Sure did, and that old geezer had a lot of power in him."

"The sorcerer must have known I had the key because he zeroed in on me like a bullet from a gun."

"Yeah, but did he want it for himself or for someone else? We need to leave by sunset. That'll give us a couple of hours to pack what we need." Wes glanced around. "We're sitting ducks here."

Jamison smiled tightly and nodded his head. "I agree."

Wes jerked Tandi behind him, causing her to stifle a scream. Her voice was barely an audible whisper. "What? More sorcerers? I'm not gonna lie; I think I've had enough adventure for one day. Scratch that—a year. This girl needs some normality. I can't wait for my pedicures on Fridays to be the big whoop-whoop."

"This day has really been great for me," Wes gloated. "My body is humming with power."

"All right, bro," I said, "We're going to need you to dial that back a bit. You look like you've stayed up all night watching porn. It's just disturbing on so many levels."

"Children, focus!" Tandi said. "Who is here?"

"No one," Jamison said after a few deep breaths. "I could sense it if someone was close."

Tandi and I watched Jamison as he veered around the crater and headed towards the woods that backed Wes's property. We all followed behind him. There, between the magnolia trees, a brightness appeared in the shadows. A tunnel of light shone from the leafy ground towards the sky.

Wes laughed. "They come to us in hologram form because they're scared of death."

Tandi gave Wes the side eye. "Well, they should be. I've known you my whole life, but seeing you swing that pole with a wicked blade on the end, while having a look on your face that screams, 'I'm a maniac that totally gets off on all the blood and pain that I'm inflicting,' is just plain creepy."

He looked over at me with a question in his eyes. I shrugged. Maybe it was a little weird but so was everything else that happened to this point. I currently lived in a glass house, so I wouldn't be throwing any stones anytime soon.

"Ladies, it's a burden that was bestowed upon me. If I try and fight it, which I have in the past, it cripples me. When a soul has expired, it is my job to claim it. What would you have me do? Pout and throw hissy fits every time I wield my scythe? Or cry like a baby every time

someone meets the end of my blade? Besides, the power rush I get is out of this world. Sue me."

The beam of light flickered, drawing all of our attention to the woods behind our house. In the dimensional image stood a man with slicked blacked hair and pale skin. His fist clenched beside his leather-clad hips. Here's the thing… men wearing leather can be done. It's like man buns. It took a special someone to pull off that look, and unfortunately he wasn't in that category. He was too skinny, and his features were almost pretty. Epic fail for him and his fashion coordinator.

There we stood, the four of us facing an image of a boy. A boy that looked at us with pure hatred.

His eyes gave me a thorough sweep before he glanced over to Jamison. "What do we have here? Prince Jamison and the mighty Undertaker working together?"

Jamison's face showed nothing but boredom. "We're all out of pleasantries. Why don't you tell us what you want before we die of boredom?"

Curiosity was killing me. "Who is this guy?"

The boy gave me a smile that was more of a leer. "Oh, I'm sorry. Where are my manners? I'm the Demon Prince who will soon be King. My sister took the crown off of my dying father's head. To be quite honest, I'm not convinced she didn't kill the old man, but none-the-less, I'll have her crown soon."

Tandi's nose wrinkled. "This is some straight up Jerry Springer stuff. I wouldn't be surprised if he said he was carrying his sister's baby."

The Demon Prince completely ignored her. "I'm here for the key. Those things really are like bartering chips.

You wouldn't believe what people are willing to do for one."

"Sorry, I think I nodded off," Wes said. "I'm sure you were trying to make a point. This is literally a snooze fest. Should we go change into our pajamas?"

"Cute." The Demon Prince studied our surroundings. "I like what you've done with the backyard. Where's the guest of honor, Warren, my infamous sorcerer?"

"You mean that weak little man that looked like a pterodactyl?" Jamison pretended to think for a second. "Oh, yes, now I recall what happened to him. He accidentally fell into a self-made pit of lava. Did you need him for something?"

"Killing my sorcerer won't get you on my good side."

Jamison and Wes both chuckled at that.

The Demon Prince was barely holding onto his anger. The vein in his temple bulged. "There was a demon who recently crossed over from a portal. After reaching out to me for sanctuary, he earned a job. He was supposed to bring me a key. My sources said he was here. Since I'm talking with the lot of you, is it safe to assume that Ellon, the demon, is no longer with us?"

"I think the more important question is why the demon would show up here with the key? Why risk it?" I asked. "A bird in the hand and all that."

"Apparently, you killed his twin brother. His revengeful nature made him disobey me and obviously got him killed. I had been forewarned he would come here; that is why I sent the sorcerer. To protect the demon who carried the key. This attack was nothing personal."

"It felt kind of personal, wouldn't you say?" Jamison asked us and we all nodded.

"Regardless, I'm going to need that key. It will give me the crown. What do I have to barter with you in order to make this happen? I can grant you anything your heart desires."

No one mentioned we didn't have possession of the key. Instead, Jamison said, "Over my dead body." Then he nodded at Wes. "Even Death will tell you that accomplishing that feat is possible, but not probable."

The Demon Prince's lips stretched over pointy teeth. Seeing he wasn't getting anywhere with the prince of wolves, he turned his attention to the Undertaker. "Have you heard the good news? The Vampire Queen is trading her daughter for a key." He wore a look of amusement. "Rumor has it that the daughter is a very powerful Zombie Queen. Sounds like a conflict of interest for you, Undertaker. I could take care of her for you."

"If you're looking for a key, why don't you just take the Vampire Queen's?" I asked.

The Demon Prince shrugged. "I was hoping this avenue would be easier."

Jamison scoffed. "Guess again."

The Demon Prince's blue eyes turned red as blood. Fury was blanketing his features. I didn't need my intuition to know that the Demon prince would bring us trouble. "I will get that key. One way or another." With his last words, his image flickered and disappeared.

"We need to get that key," I said to no one in particular. "Where did that pit of lava lead?"

Jamison answered. "My guess? To the Underworld. Sorcerers can't open portals, but they can open the gates to other dimensions like Hell. Good thing your brother can close the gate."

"Hell is my playground, little sister," Wes said. "I can retrieve the key, but then after that I have business to attend to."

I looked at my big brother and studied his determined profile. "What kind of business?"

"I have to go find this Zombie Queen and kill her," Wes said.

I slapped him on his shoulder. "You can't just kill an innocent girl!"

"Seriously?" He smiled at me. "I've heard of this 'innocent girl.' She's a vampire princess and a zombie queen all wrapped up in one. There's nothing innocent about her."

Jamison pointed out, "If she's evil, and he doesn't do what is necessary, she could make it hard on us to win the war."

"Oh, for the love of everything fried, I'm going to bed. Today has been exhausting," Tandi said with mock disgust. "I don't care if we're safe here or not, I'm not moving from this house. It seems to me no matter where we go, danger will be there." Tandi walked toward our house. "And I have a date with Netflix and a fluffy couch. Zombie vampire queens, flying bird-men, and crazy witches can all take a back seat for a hot minute. I'm tired."

Wes chuckled. "If y'all will excuse me, I have a date with a warmer climate." Smoke gathered around him before he completely disappeared to go find the key.

"Then there were two." Jamison wrapped both arms around me. "I'm sorry for not telling you about your brother."

"Just no more secrets, okay?" I traced his five o'clock shadow. "You know, I could get use to this scruffy look."

"You like, huh?" He bent his head toward mine, slowly kissing me on each side of my mouth before kissing me squarely on the lips. As he deepened the kiss, my body melted into his. All of a sudden, the kiss ended with Jamison pushing my body from his and roughly shoving me behind him. I was still in a daze, wondering what was going on with my angel when I heard a noise in front of us. I peered around Jamison and was shocked at what I saw. Mother trucker. Could we not have a moment of peace?

chapter eighteen

There stood the biggest demon we had yet to see so far. He was at least eight feet tall with bulging muscles and horns sticking out from his head. An instant later, the demon transformed into a middle-aged man wearing a suit. Now, he looked completely boring, with mousy brown hair that was receding and pallid skin. I blinked a couple of times to make sure that what I just saw really happened and wasn't just a figment of my imagination.

The man smiled. "Hello, Prince." He nodded at me. "Witch."

Jamison all but growled, letting me know this wasn't a friendly visit. "How long have you been on this plain, François?"

"Too long. A demon has needs that cannot really be met here." He leered at me, giving me chills. "She is beautiful, like her mother."

I felt Jamison tense. "Why are you here?"

"I think you know why. You've really pissed off the boss man. The demon prince sent me to retrieve his key."

"That's going to be a problem, considering I don't have it."

"Well, that is a problem for you." He eyed Jamison with a calculating look. "Tell me who does."

Jamison shrugged. "I can't really remember his name off the top of my head."

The demon smirked right before I felt an invisible force tug me toward him like a magnet. My arms were pinned helplessly at my sides; I looked down to see what was constricting me. There were tiny wisps of gray vapors, almost like tiny hands, holding onto me, wrapping me in a tight vise. My body was trapped against the demon in less than a second. Then from thin air, a silver dagger with foreign words embellished on the side materialized in the demon's hand, halting Jamison from moving closer to us.

"Good wolf." The demon put the cold blade underneath my chin. "Before you use any powers, doll face, you need to know that one small cut from this blade and your blood will be poisoned. The only way you can cleanse yourself from the curse of my blade is by me removing the curse. Otherwise, you will die. Do you understand?"

Careful not to move too much against his blade, I said, "Perfectly."

"Great. Now, wolf, you know how this works?"

Jamison tightened his fists. "If you hurt her, I will kill you in the worst possible way."

The demon laughed out loud. "That is rich. You think you can do anything to me that hasn't been done before?"

"I've been told I'm very imaginative. I'm sure I could come up with something excruciating and original. What is it you want me to do, François?"

Terror wrapped around me in an iron grip like a python squeezing its prey. My breath felt like it was being squeezed out of me as the demon applied pressure, and the blade cut into my neck, drawing blood. He bent his head toward me, and I could feel his nostrils flaring against my sensitive skin. "Oopsie. I think I slipped. Can you smell that from there, Prince? Even with her blood now being tainted, she still smells divine. Mortals, they are so fragile, aren't they?"

As blood dribbled down my neck, I panicked. Was this how I died? How long did I have to live?

Jamison's hands were clenched so tight I could see the veins bulging in his arms. "I will kill you for this."

"You will try," the demon replied.

"I will succeed. Tell me what you want."

The demon eased up on my neck, and I closed my eyes in relief. "I want the key, of course. The Underworld has been an extra level of Hell with the Demon Prince trying to figure a way to overthrow his sister. I can win favor with our soon-to-be, newly crowned king if I can obtain the key. You will have twenty-four hours to give me the key, or you forfeit her life." The demon nuzzled my neck, and bile rose in my stomach. "You know my name. All you have to do is say it out loud and I'll come."

More grey wisps covered my body, and then I was standing alone. The demon was gone as fast as he'd come.

"Are you all right, love?" Jamison asked, running a gentle hand over my neck. I felt the bleeding stop under his fingertips.

No. No, I wasn't all right. My brother would be collecting my soul if he didn't soon return with that key.

"Can all demons come and go like that?" That was a scary thought. I would never be able to close my eyes in the shower again.

"No. They can't. That blade he carries has power."

As he cradled me in his arms, I asked, "What do we do now?"

He held my head to his chest and said, "I go after the key."

"But my brother's gone after it. He might have already found it by now and is on his way back."

Jamison squeezed me to him. "What if he hasn't found it yet? What if he gets waylaid? I can't risk all the 'what if's,' Charlie."

I looked over nervously at the hole in the ground. "Entering Hell will hurt you, won't it?"

"Yeah, but it won't kill me. You would never survive the first realm of Hell, so that's why you have to stay here. I'll be back before you know it."

What if he didn't come back? A sharp stabbing pain hit my heart. I was in love with the prince of wolves. Somewhere along the way, I had come to rely on his presence. It was something I couldn't fully explain, but I needed him. Trying to keep my emotions in check, I said, "Come back to me in one piece."

"And if I don't, then it's no biggie. I regenerate at a fast speed."

"Smart-aleck, you know what I meant."

Pulling me to him, he bit my bottom lip before kissing me thoroughly. "I will always come back to you."

Somehow, I knew he meant those words, and that in itself was encouraging. "Wes probably closed the gate behind him. How are you going to get to Hell?"

"Easy. I know the Demon Princess; well, I guess she is the queen now—I know her full name. I'll summon her and explain to her about her brother double-crossing her. I'll give her my promise to kill him myself if she allows me safe travels throughout the Underworld."

"What the hell? I was gone for ten minutes, and you've already attracted another demon?" We turned around to see a disheveled Wes with smudges on his face, burnt places on his arms, and holes in his clothes.

I ran over to him. "What happened?" My hands reached out and patted his still smoldering shirt.

"What do you mean, what happened? I went to Hell and back." He leaned his head forward, dusting ashes out of his hair. "I've sent a lot of souls to Hell, and nobody wants a reminder of why they're there in the Underworld. Let's just say, I had a highly aggressive welcoming committee waiting at the gate for my arrival."

"Did you get the key?" Jamison asked.

I stared at my older brother in amazement as I watched his wounds heal right in front of my face.

"What the hell kind of question is that?" Wes said. "Of course, I did. I had to wrestle it away from a troll. You know how that goes. He didn't want to let go of his treasure. I ended up throwing my watch at him to distract him. It was a damn good watch, too."

"We need to call that demon, so he can remove the curse," Jamison said.

"Whoa! What?" Wes asked.

I told Wes of the demon who showed up in his backyard. After I was done, Jamison added, "Not just any knife. It was the dagger used by Abadiar."

"The what of who?" I asked.

Jamison said, "Abadiar is, or was, one of the most powerful under lords in the Underworld. There are twelve under lords reigning under the King or Queen in this case. He's under lord of the Western part of Hell. He rules, or ruled, with a very magical dagger. With one wave, the dagger can call thousands of demon soldiers to his side in an instant." Jamison ran a hand over his stubble. "So if François has the dagger, it means he's taken out Abadiar and is now the lord of the West. Which explains why he reeked of power and was so sure of himself."

"I assume you have a plan?" Wes asked.

"He said we had to give him the key. He didn't say we had to let him keep it. I'm going to give him the key, and then we'll take it back from him. We have twenty-four hours to come up with something before the curse sets in."

We were all quiet for a second. It seemed like this was our fate. Get the key, lose the key.

"So when we're ready, we just call out his name?" I asked.

"Something like that," Jamison said.

Wes threw an arm around me. "I'm the Undertaker. I would know if you had an expiration date above your head. You are not going to die. Everything will be fine."

But would it? We all headed back towards the house. I didn't feel like I had been cursed, but I knew that the under lord didn't lie about my fate. I didn't want to summon him and perhaps his army, but I also didn't want to die. I briefly made eye contact with Jamison before I averted my gaze. His eyes told me what I already knew. He cared for me deeply. It was written all over his face and I couldn't stomach the thought of leaving him. I'm too weary to pretend that this thing between us is just an attraction. It's deeper. His hand reached out and snagged mine.

He waited for Wes to get far ahead of us before he said, "It will be okay."

I felt my eyes water. "How do you know?"

He closed his eyes for a moment before he spoke. "Because I can't lose you."

This time I was ready for his kiss. His mouth crushed mine telling me exactly what he was feeling without ever saying a word. When he released me were both panting for air. My head dropped to his chest where he murmured sweet words while stroking my hair. I had to believe that everything would work out because I couldn't bear the thought of leaving him. If we could just secure the key–but every time we got close to it, we lost it. I was starting to think it was never ours to keep.

chapter nineteen

The first thing I did when I got in the house was ask everyone for a moment alone then I excused myself so that I could have a mental breakdown. I headed straight for the upstairs bath in hopes I would have no witnesses. With the way our luck had been running, there would be some kind of Degenerate showing up soon, looking to maim or kill one or all of us. I didn't care what kind of evil came knocking on his door. The next forty-five minutes were reserved for me soaking in the tub because I deserved a little downtime, damn it to hell.

As I soaked in the tub, I thought about what the kids at school would say if they knew I was a witch. Flicking a bubble with my toe, I smiled. Tandi was probably already making a list of things she wanted me to do to Jenny, to hone my craft, of course, not because she loathed the girl or anything. There were five more months left of my senior year, but going back to school seemed impossible now. How did one sit and listen to anyone teach about history when the future hung in the balance? If this curse was lifted from me and there was a tomorrow for me, I wasn't completely sure what my future held, but my gut

said it involved Jamison. It also told me that I was going to have a part in helping the Lux secure the second key.

Climbing out of the bathtub, I quickly got dressed in a clean pair of jeans and a tank top. I didn't know the proper attire when calling a demon under-lord and I didn't care. I walked down the stairs and quietly opened the study doors where a snoring Tandi was sprawled out on the couch. Pulling a quilt over her shoulders, I said a silent prayer that she would stay asleep through this whole summoning-a-demon thing. She had been traumatized enough for one day. I closed the doors behind me and headed for the living room where I heard voices.

Wes stood five feet away from Jamison, each of them flanking the fireplace. It was amazing how one looked like an avenging angel and the other like hell on wheels, and yet both were deliverers of death.

Wes was saying, "I send people to Hell. I don't receive visitors from the Underworld. This is a whole new concept for me."

"Well, what do we do now?" I asked. "Figure out a way to get the key and then keep it from any sorcerers, demons, or fake hologram-y people?"

Wes winked. "You forgot about vampires, werewolves, fairies, and—"

"Just stop." I held up a hand. "First things first. Let's make a plan for this under lord."

Wes stood up. "I need to grab something. I'll be right back."

"We need a containment circle. It will enable us to call him and keep him right where we want him until he lifts the curse. He won't lift the curse until he has the key," Jamison explained.

"So, someone will have to be in the circle with him to snag the key back. He won't expect much from me, so I'm the one who should be in the circle."

"No," Jamison said.

I turned away from the fireplace. "Excuse me?"

"I said no. That's dangerous. You would be nothing more than bait. I can't just sit back and let you go in that circle alone."

"Jamison, Wes already said that I wasn't going to die."

"There are some things worse than death, Charlie," Jamison said.

Wes strolled into the living room. "There are underground passages that allow non-demons to go below. If the demon takes you to the Underworld, we will get to you, but who knows what he'll do to you before we find you," Wes said. "Demons are sadistic creatures and the shadows… They're enough to break an immortal, much less a human, even if you are a powerful witch."

"Well, then don't let him take me, boys."

Wes said, "There's something I want to show you before we start. I think it'll help you." He handed me an old book fraying around the edges. It smelled dusty, and the fabric had unidentifiable stains on it. "Here, take it. I would have given it to you a lot sooner, but you weren't ready."

"What is this old thing?"

"I was up in the attic where all my canvases are, and as I was moving some empty boxes around, I found this old book laying on top of a memento box—basically, our christening blankets and some other things that only a mother would treasure. This book—"

"Was Mom's?" I knew that it was. I could feel an immediate attachment to the old, dusty thing.

"Yeah. Before we call this demon, I wanted you to have it." My eyes rounded. "No, not because I think you're going to die, and I want you to have something special before you kick the bucket, but I just thought you would want to know more. More about her. More about you."

Jamison nodded at Wes. "That was kind of you."

I curled up on the couch with the book in my lap. "Aww, a bromance in the making. Love it. Now, both of you go somewhere else while I skim through this."

Jamison nodded. "I'll get your brother to help me with the circle, and we'll call you when we're ready."

I was already opening my mother's book, so I ignored them both as they headed towards the kitchen. As my hands touched the pages, my gut tightened. Tears welled in my eyes, and I could feel power. My mother's power. It was as if my fingers were touching a piece of her. As the edges of the book started to ice, I made myself take some deep, calming breaths. I flipped the pages until I got to page one hundred thirty-nine. That page called to me. After a short paragraph explaining that every powerful witch needed a familiar, it went on like a recipe. It even had the degree of difficulty it would take to make the spell.

It seemed like a simple spell, really. I needed to put the book down and focus on the task at hand. We had so much to prepare for, but my intuition was telling me I needed this spell, and I needed it now. Looking at the directions, it called for a personal item from me and a lock of my hair. I took off the ruby ring my brother had given me on my seventeenth birthday and placed it on the coffee table. After locating a pair of scissors on an old bookshelf, I cut a small lock of my hair from the underneath. I grabbed a bowl and then set both items in it and placed the bowl on the coffee table. As I gathered the book back into my arms, I got chill bumps. This was crazy. I should be in the kitchen with the boys, asking them how they planned on lifting my curse and scoring the key. But no, I was trying to cast my first spell for a cat. At least, I guessed it would be a cat. Weren't all witch's familiars a cat? I began to read. There were a couple of seconds of an inner war with myself… Did I perform the spell knowing I would be heavily tied to it? A spell that I had no clue how it would turn out? I closed the book with frustration and immediately felt saddened. I needed that familiar! Oh, what the hell. I grabbed the book again, flipping back to the page I was looking for.

My lips started moving as I chanted the words, and an intense feeling I could only describe as intoxicating started to bubble up within me, and as quickly as that seeded power came, it swiftly exited. Now, I was to light the lock of hair on fire. With a wave of my hand—I was getting so good at that—I set my hair on fire. Not wanting to ruin my ring, I contained the fire just to my lock of hair. After the thickness in the air dissipated, I looked around the room for my familiar. There was nothing. Hmm, maybe I short-circuited or got the spell wrong?

Minutes went by and nothing. Well, so much for that. Disappointment flooded me. I would try again after we summoned the demon. I went to stand when all of a sudden, a two-foot leprechaun jumped on my lap, as in a pot of gold at the end of the rainbow freakin' leprechaun. Before I could gather my wits and scream, he sprinkled some dust, sealing my lips together.

"Unh, unh, unh. I'm not here to hurt you, so no bloody screaming. It hurts my delicate ears. Agree?"

I nodded, and he waved his arm, freeing my lips. I studied the man, or thing, sitting on my lap. He was cute in a uniquely striking way with his wavy, whitish-blond locks that touched his shoulders and sparkling gray eyes. He was eerie, but his chubby little cheeks softened the creep factor.

After finally finding my voice, I asked, "Are you a… a leprechaun?"

His eyes narrowed, and he crossed his arms over his broad chest. "Do I sound like I come from Ireland, girly? And don't let my short stature throw you for a loop. This is the image I choose to project. It's the one I'm most comfortable with. Leprechaun, my butt."

This was what happened when exhaustion finally took over: I started hallucinating. "I am… I am so sorry. I didn't mean to offend you. I'm just so new to all of this, and it was my best guess. Honest to goodness, I apologize for upsetting you."

If I thought he was upset a second ago, I was about to be in for a real treat. His whole body twitched with anger, and his face turned the color of a beet. Hallucination or not, this midget scared the bejeebies out of me. I started eyeing the distance to the door. Could I somehow alert the boys before this creature silenced me again?

"Don't even think about it, witch. Your powers are immense, but it's apparent that you don't know squat about who you are or what you're capable of, so until then, I trump you. Upset me? First, you call me one of those lying, cheating scoundrels who would stab their own mother in the back if the pay was good enough, then you apologize for upsetting me. What am I, a twelve-year-old girl?" He hopped off my lap and began to pace in front of me with his short little legs. "Just think of me as your more than awesome familiar. I've been created to guard you, guide you, and to help you in any way I can. Obviously, we'll need to start training you right away on how to use your abilities." He stroked his baby face. "The spell bringing me here was a complicated one, and yet you did it within mere minutes. With that kind of power, you could accidentally blow up the whole South if you didn't know how to harness it properly."

"Oh, well, I definitely wouldn't want to do that."

"Well, of course not." He stopped pacing to give me a befuddled look. "I can tell some big magic is happening in the next room. You planning on summoning a demon, girly?"

"It's kind of a long story—"

"Well, we don't really have time for long stories, do we?" He jumped up on my lap again. If he had issues with crossing personal boundaries, he wasn't showing it. "Sorry, girly. It's a tad uncomfortable when your familiar reads your mind for the first time."

Before I could say anything, his thick fingers were cupping my face, and I sucked in a breath as my head started to ache. Just when I didn't think I could take any more, he pulled back.

"Just as I feared. We're in deep muck, and you're as clueless as a newborn babe."

Starting to take offense with this small Keebler elf, I said, "Whoa, I'm not completely clueless. I can call fire, wind, fog, and ice, and if you really are here to help me, how about you pony up and show me a way I can get uncursed and maintain possession of the key, so I can help save the world, instead of telling me how inadequate I am?"

"You're right. Apologies. The things you listed as your attributes could be considered awesome if you weren't the queen of the freaking witches! Bugger it all." He took a couple of deep breaths. "Girly, you've got so much more up your sleeve. Would you like to see what your ancestors were capable of?"

I looked towards the kitchen. Why hadn't Jamison or Wes come in yet?

"Oh, you don't know what you've done do you?"

"Um…"

His chubby hands patted my cheeks. "You can freeze things. Now that you've got your amazingly awesome familiar, you've unlocked more power." At my confused expression, he waved a hand. "You literally froze time."

"What?" I shouted. Pushing him off my lap, I ran to the kitchen. Jamison was frozen in place, even the salt he was using to make a circle stilled in the air. My brother's eyes were moving, but his feet were planted.

The little man came up beside me. "Well, that bloke will be unfrozen soon. No one can really freeze death."

What had I done? This was bad. "How do I undo this?"

"Simple. You will them to unfreeze." I concentrated but nothing happened. "Yeah, okay, how about you think of them moving once again?"

I did as he asked. Jamison and Wes immediately moved, and both looked at me.

"What just happened," Jamison asked, "and who the hell are you?"

The small man's bushy, pale eyebrows drew together. "Hello, rudeness. I'm Samuel. My friends call me Sammy. I, unlike you, need no introductions, considering I operate at a higher level of thinking." He pointed at Wes, then Jamison. "Brother, and you, golden boy, are her—"

Jamison all but growled, "Familiar, is it? Do you have a death wish?"

"What's he talking about?" I asked.

"Yeah, what's he talking about?" Wes said with enough menace in his voice to make me swallow hard.

Samuel's eyes twinkled with mischief. "Oops. Dear me. What have I done? Unfortunately, we don't have time for Days of Our Sucky Lives; our girl here only has hours to live. I'm sure you both can smell the poison running through her now. May I suggest a plan? One that will cure the curse, help you to obtain the key, and give you the blade to have in your possession, so this doesn't happen again?"

I wanted to know why Jamison looked like he was about to hurt my new familiar, and why my brother was glaring at Jamison. But the need to hear Sammy's plan outweighed any drama. I would figure it all out as soon as I dealt with this demon.

As Sammy explained, I felt my mood lightening. This was a plan I could roll with. Sammy finally turned to me with a question in his eyes, and my only answer was a smile. The most powerful demon was coming here to my brother's house, and I was more afraid for him than me. He might hold the key momentarily, but in the end, we would have ownership of it. We were definitely going to win this war.

fter Sammy explained to the three of us what I was truly capable of, we all had more confidence in summoning the demon. An intricate symbol covered the kitchen floor. Candles were lit all around. Tandi, unfortunately, woke up. I was hoping we could be rid of the demon and secure the key while she slept, but fate had decided otherwise. My friend was yawning as she entered the kitchen still looking exhausted, despite the long nap she took. Squeezing her hand, I explained to her about the demon that was about to give us a house call and how I had acquired a familiar.

Sammy came up behind Tandi and lightly pinched her on the bottom. She yelped and swatted him upside his head. There she stood, nostrils flaring, taking in every tiny inch of Sammy before she turned to me. "One of two things are going to happen in my future, and no, I didn't have to talk to a soothsayer to find out. I'm either going to need intensive therapy, or I'm turning to drugs, and I mean like hardcore drugs because I don't do anything half-ass."

Totally understanding her feelings, I nodded sympathetically. "So Sammy, this is my best friend, Tandi, and if you value your man parts, you should probably keep your hands to yourself from here on out. Tandi, this is Sammy, my familiar."

One blonde eyebrow arched. "So, he's like your personal assistant? Awesome, go get me some sweet tea, little man."

I prepared myself for the indignation Sammy was inevitably going to rain down on Tandi, but instead, he said, "Sure thing, my beautiful queen."

Sammy handed Tandi her glass of tea, and she didn't bother to thank him. She yawned loudly. Even rumpled from sleep, she still looked like a diva. She put a hand on a curvy hip. "I'm assuming as long as I'm outside of this circle, I'll be good?"

Jamison nodded. "Yes."

I rubbed my hands together with excitement. "Let's do this."

Wes leaned up against a wall. "If I didn't know better, little sister, I would say you're almost eager to summon François."

Jamison pulled me into him and rested his chin on top of my head. "Just don't forget that he is a demon wielding a mighty blade."

"I know, I know. He's big, bad, and scary. And if he takes me with him, he'll probably do unthinkable things to me before you can rescue me. I understand."

Jamison shook his head. "If he's able to take you to the Underworld with him, I swear to you that I will find you."

"That's a big promise," Wes said. "If he takes her to his kingdom, it will be like breaking into Fort Knox. You would have to kill thousands of demons just to reach her."

"Totally doable." Jamison stared straight at me. "It's a promise I aim to keep. Let's get this over with."

Sammy made a noise between a snort and hiccup. "You might be the strongest of your kind, wolf, but she's the strongest of her kind. She might just surprise you."

"Hey, nothing Charlie does surprises me anymore," Tandi said. "Not even when I wake up to find her own version of a Smurf following her around."

Sammy wiggled his white eyebrows. "Baby, I could turn blue for you if you wanted me to. You could even call me Papa."

My familiar got all out of sorts when I called him a leprechaun, but Tandi can call him a Smurf, and he's totally okay with that. Whatever.

"Nice." Tandi took a sip of tea. "He's a perv. He'll fit right in with our inner circle, and by that, I mean you and me."

Laughing, I hugged Tandi and patted Sammy on the head before stepping into the circle. Sniffles came from behind me. "Don't cry, Tandi. I'll make it out in one piece."

Tandi dried her eyes. "If you don't, I'm killing your brother and Jamison. I wouldn't know what to do without you." She sobbed the last part.

Wes snorted. "If you actually found a way to kill me, you would inherit my line of work, and that would definitely interfere with your shopping schedule."

"Okay, okay. Let's begin," I intervened before Tandi could give us a list of the people she would kill first if she was the Undertaker.

After receiving a nod from Wes, I stepped into the middle of the circle. I never broke eye contact with Jamison while I listened to Wes summon the demon. Jamison looked like he wanted to prevent me from going through with this, but there was something else in his eyes too… pride. Gradually, the air pressure started to change, and the room temperature rose to a sweltering degree. It slowly got harder and harder to breathe.

I heard the demon's deep laughter before I saw him. This time around, François decided to forgo the appearance of the middle-aged man and came to us in full-blown demon form, horns and all. He took a moment to observe his surroundings before grabbing hold of my elbow, pulling me to him.

The demon eyed the key in Wes's hand. "I assume that's my key?"

Wes lightly tossed the key toward Jamison, who snagged it in midair.

"Remove her curse, and I vow to you that I will throw you the key," Jamison said.

"I have heard stories of you, Prince, and I am beyond flabbergasted that you would so easily allow me to have the key." The demon smiled. "So I will say this, no harm will come to her by my hand as long as I have the key."

"Touching. Remove the curse," Wes snarled.

François spoke in a foreign language before his blade turned burnt orange. Smoke started to rise from the blade. I knew what he intended a moment before he pressed the hot blade to my skin, but it still didn't prepare me for the intense, searing pain. I bit my lip to keep from crying out. Finally, the blade cooled as he finished speaking.

"There, I vow that she is curse-free. Now, toss me the key."

Jamison threw the key to the demon, who caught it one handed.

The air pressure started to change again, and before our eyes, another demon appeared to the right of François.

The smaller demon bowed his head before François. "Massster, you called?"

François shoved me towards the other demon. "I made a vow, Prince, that I wouldn't hurt your little dove if you gave me the key, but I made no promises of what my minions would do."

Tandi screamed at Wes to do something, but he was already running towards me, as if he could get to me before the demon disappeared with me into the Underworld. Big brother didn't have faith or so it would seem. I glanced over to Jamison who stood stock still. He gave me a small nod.

Sammy shouted, "Now or never, girl!"

I took a deep breath and prayed I didn't botch this plan. Our only plan. I opened my eyes and looked around. I saw the people I love frozen in place, including Wes, although his thumb was twitching. Both demons stood frozen in time, wearing sneers.

I quickly grabbed the key out of François's hand. Then I rummaged in his mustard-colored trousers and found the blade of Abadiar. As soon as my skin made contact with the blade, I yelped in pain. I dropped the blade and looked at my burnt hand. Welts covered my fingertips. Kneeling down, I waved a hand over the blade, freezing it into a block of ice before picking it back up. Making sure I didn't disturb the salt, I stepped out of the circle, carrying both objects. Once I was clear of the demons, I released my hold.

Jamison leaned over and kissed me on top of the head. "Good job."

"What just happened?" François demanded.

"We gave you the key," I said. "But then we took it back. I also took your blade. Hope you don't mind."

"Why you little—"

Wes wagged a finger. "Now, now, François, it's not nice to insult a lady. Especially when she has you by the balls."

"Fine, you win that round." François clapped. "It looks as if your little witch has been holding out on us. A power like freezing time is scarce. Can you imagine what a hit she will be in the Underworld? Who knows? I might even let her rule by my side, if she proves herself to be worthy."

The tension in the air was thick. "That will never happen," Jamison growled.

"I'll have to disagree with you, Prince," the demon said.

"Over my dead body."

The demon grinned as he looked over at Wes. "What do you say, Undertaker? Does your new-found friend have an expiration date above his head?"

"No. But you have one above yours. I wonder how you'll die, François? Hopefully, I'll be right there to claim your soul, so that I can re-send you to Hell. I can almost taste the power I'll have harvesting an under lord."

Whether Wes was bluffing or not, I wasn't sure, but François showed a moment of alarm, before he masked the fear on his face. "I won't forget this. In fact, I—"

Jamison sighed. "Can't you make him go away?"

Wes laughed. "It seems you've bored everyone, François. I command you to return to the Underworld."

François's shouts were incoherent as he went back to wherever he came from faster than the eye could track. Good riddance!

"Sweet." Wes came over and took the block of ice from me. "I'll be adding this bad boy to the collection of cool stuff I've confiscated so far. Um, could you unfreeze it, though?"

I waved a hand over the blade. The water hit the floor, and I waited for my brother to drop the blade in pain as I did. But that never happened. He turned the blade over and over in his hand, examining it. Ugh, so not fair.

Jamison's nose flared. "You're hurt."

"Obviously the stupid blade has a different effect on me than it does on dear, ol' brother." He took my hand in his, and within seconds it was feeling better. "Thank you."

He responded by kissing my hand.

Tandi rubbed her arms. "Will they be back?"

"Maybe," Jamison answered. "But if we kill an under lord without being attacked first, we would have entered in a war against the Queen of Demons. And just so that we're clear, Undertaker, I'll be the one taking François's life if he comes anywhere near Charlie."

"As long as he dies a slow death, I couldn't care less who delivers the final blow." Wes winked at Tandi. "Come on, girl, let's go watch some of your vampire shows on Netflix."

Poor Tandi was exhausted, but she put up a brave front. "I do have a thing for vampires."

"I'm totally knackered," Sammy said. "I'm going to find a warm bed to sleep in. Don't disturb me, or I'll cast a spell on the lot of you."

I studied Sammy as his chubby little legs walked up the steps. My gut told me he couldn't cast spells, but I made a mental note not to wake the little man just in case. My familiar was a cranky thing.

Jamison was studying the key he now had in his hand. Several different emotions flitted across his face as he rotated the black object in his palm. As soon as Tandi and Wes had left the room, I asked, "What about the key? Where will you hide it? You should probably hide it quickly before we lose it… again." I was halfway joking. Kind of.

"I have the perfect place for it," Jamison said. "Let's rest a bit, and you can help me put the key where it belongs."

I smiled as I put my hand in his. He made it seem as if we were still a team. He could have taken the key and left. That was why he came here to begin with, but instead he was still here, holding my hand. My heart squeezed, and I was sure stupid pheromones were releasing from me left and right. My body was a traitor. We stood there staring at each other before one corner of his mouth lifted into one of the sexiest grins I'd ever had the pleasure of witnessing. He gave my hand a little tug, and I followed him into the living room.

Tandi had exchanged her fancy dress for a pair of Wes's sweatpants and an old high-school basketball shirt and was now sprawled out in a recliner. "Wes, once a demon is dead, does it just return to Hell?"

"To live? No. Everyone goes to an afterlife. If the demon is evil, it will return to Hell, but not to rule or be ruled. Dead is dead, no matter what being you are."

"Awesome," I said. "So if he attacks us and we kill him, then we'll never have to deal with him again."

"Right," answered Jamison as he flopped on the couch next to me. "Here's to hoping he attacks."

Tandi grabbed the remote. "Question, are vampires in the real world as hot as they are on television?"

Jamison wore a look of disgust. "Did you really just ask two dudes that?"

Tandi huffed. "Hmm, I think I got my answer. If they were butt-ugly, y'all would've said something about them being hideous creatures and then fist-bumped each other to show your hot male superiority."

Both men laughed, and there we all sat, resting for the first time in what seemed like ages in a living room that looked like it had survived a mild earthquake. I was curse free. Wes had a blade to add to his collection, and most importantly we had the key. It was a long, hard road, but we finally had the key, and the icing on the cake was we were all alive to brag about it.

chapter twenty one

t some point, I must have dozed off on Jamison's shoulder. The doorbell rang, startling me out of a deep sleep. I wiped my mouth silently, cheering when there wasn't any drool. I shook Tandi awake, and now all four of us looked at each other. I finally broke the silence. "What kind of hellfire and brimstone demon uses the front door?"

Jamison cocked his head to the side. "It's not a demon, love. It's a vampire."

He got up from the couch and opened the door, and I had an image overload. I don't know what stunned me more, the gorgeous man or the beautiful girl standing beside him.

Jamison nodded to both of them. "I recognize the neck biter, but you are?"

The girl dressed in all black stumbled in through the doorway, mumbling something about how she wished Ariana had kept her mouth shut, and how she wasn't meant for swampy territory. "Jolene. My nickname is Jo."

The gothic-looking chic was otherworldly beautiful, but was acting crazy as she not only asked herself questions, but then answered them. She was five feet two with jet-black hair that was cut longer in the front, framing her heart-shaped face.

Her electric blue eyes widened as she noticed her audience staring at her. She gave me a frustrated smile. "Sorry, I know my manners are bad, but where I'm from, there are no mosquitoes the size of my hand, humidity that clings to you like a vine, or reptiles lurking in all bodies of water. This landscape is enough to make a girl mental. Plus, I have the gift of sight, so I'm already a tad mental. Buuuut I'm trying to learn how to control it, even though right now it's like a Tsunami of visions hitting me. One right after another."

Jamison pulled me closer to him. I was ninety percent sure he thought the girl just escaped the loony bin. "I'm Jamison, and this is Charlie."

I gave a little finger wave. "Hello."

She shooed us with a hand. "Yes, yes, I know. I have sight, remember?"

The vampire wasn't paying any attention to the strange girl. He reached out a hand to me, and I studied the man in front of me through my eyelashes. With his brown hair and dark chocolate eyes, he looked every inch of a Calvin Klein advertisement.

"My name is Stephan. And you are an extraordinary beauty." I thought he was going to shake my hand, but instead he flipped it over and kissed the back. I had a feeling his charming demeanor was all part of an act.

Jamison growled, "Get your hands off of her before you get staked."

I could have sworn Stephan was taunting Jamison. Pulling my hand away from the vampire in hopes of deflating the hostile environment, I cleared my throat. "Nice to meet you," I heard myself saying because "why the heck are you here?" seemed so rude.

Jolene rolled her eyes. "Please ignore Stephan. He likes to rile Jamison and his brother. I guess when you're one of the oldest vampires in the world, you get bored easily if you're not creating havoc everywhere you go."

Sammy came bounding down the steps. "Thanks for telling me we had company." He stopped on the last step. "Annnnd that's a vampire." He rubbed a hand down his chest circling a nipple once. "Tell me fanger, does this appeal to you?"

The vampire looked disgusted. "Not even remotely."

"Cool, mate. Just checking." Sammy went over to where Tandi was sitting. "What about you beautiful?"

Tandi was quiet for a second. "Oh, I'm sorry. Did you really expect me to answer that?"

Stephan moved toward her like a lion stalking an antelope. His nose flared as he reached out and tugged on a golden strand of her hair. His eyes roamed over every inch of Tandi, as his brows raised an inch on his forehead. She stood stock still as he gazed at her with such intensity it even made me uncomfortable. He muttered something I couldn't hear but had Jamison and Wes shuffling their feet.

"Um… this is awkward," Tandi said, laughing nervously.

Jolene yawned loudly, tapping her foot. "Stephan, please step away from the girl. You're kind of giving off the creepy, yet hot vibe. Dial it back a bit."

"Dang vampires, can't take em' nowhere," Sammy said. "Bloody wanker."

Wes stood up and put himself between the vampire and Tandi. Stephan finally shook himself out of his thoughts long enough to glance at my brother. "Well, what do we have here? The Undertaker, himself."

"Should I start wearing a name tag?" Wes addressed the whole group. "I'm not really much of an entertainer, partly due to the fact that I don't like people. It's the main reason I never invite anyone to my house, and the last time I checked, I didn't send out invitations, so why are you here, and what's the fastest way to get you both to leave?"

"Excuse my brother." I gave him a 'please don't be rude' glare. "He has social anxiety problems." I glanced over at Jolene because the crazy girl was easier to look at than the intense, hot vampire, who was still studying Tandi with a puzzling expression. "Why are you here exactly?"

Jolene smacked her forehead, and the mumbling began tenfold, then her eyes cleared, and she sighed. She tapped a finger to her head. "Jeez, I wish I could turn off the switchboard for a second. Did you ask a question? Yes, I remember. We're here because Ariana—the one who's training me—the head honcho of soothsayers and sight bringers told us that it was imperative Stephan and I be here tonight." She nibbled on her lip. "I'm going to be totally transparent. I don't really have any control over my visions as of yet, so I've only seen bits and pieces of what's to come. Until I learn more control, all the voices in my head kind of make me a little batty."

"You don't say," Wes said.

I cut him another glare. Not that it would do any good.

Jolene clapped her hands. "So, you got the key?"

Jamison's arms tightened around me, and I looked up into my angel's face. He smiled at me, showing dimples that made me weak in the knees. "Yeah, we secured it. Charlie here actually did it all by herself. She also stole the blade of Abadiar from an under lord."

"You're joking?" Stephan said.

Jamison laughed at the perplexed look on the vampire's face. "Nope. She's something else."

"That blade is thousands of years old. I was actually there when it was made."

Tandi's mouth fell open. "Are all of you freakishly old, too? I mean, does anyone here know Moses?"

The vampire chuckled. "Jolene is not that old, are you, Jo?"

We all looked at Jolene, who was currently staring off into space. It was like her body was here, but her mind was far away. I heard Sammy mumble, "Oh crap," right before Jolene's body convulsed.

The vampire was quick to catch her before she hit the ground. He carried her over to an armchair. After several minutes, Jolene looked slightly embarrassed as she asked, "Sorry. Did I miss much?"

"What did you see, Jo?" The vampire asked.

She swallowed. "There are many coming. They will be here before dawn." She glanced at all of us, one by one until her gaze stopped on Tandi. "Some of us will not make it."

"You mean, Tandi?" I shouted.

"I am so sorry." Jolene walked over to where Tandi sat on the couch, taking the seat next to her. "Even if we try and hide you someplace safe, François will find you. You were here when Charlie outmaneuvered him at his own game. It hurt his ego that he was bested. He knows killing the Prince and the Undertaker is almost impossible, but he has already formulated a plan of action—one that has both of you girls caught up in the middle of all of this."

Tandi cupped her ear with her hand. "I'm sorry, girl. I don't think I heard you right. Are you telling me that I'll be dead soon?"

My voice shook. "No. There is no way that we're going to just give up and die."

Jolene gazed at me with pity. "I didn't say that I foresaw you dying, Charlie." Her eyes jerked to Tandi once again before settling back to me. "Some things are worse than death. You will have your own problems, Charlie."

My heart dropped into the pit of my stomach. "Well, I'll be damned if I just sit around and let my best friend die. Or let some demon torture me." I swiveled to face my brother. "And wouldn't you of all people know if Tandi was about to die?"

"It appeared an hour ago," my brother said sheepishly.

"Damn it to hell, Wes. When did you think it'd be a good time to tell us?"

"After I figured it out! I'm not carrying her soul over, and I'm not letting anyone else take her either." He started pacing the floor.

Jamison spun me around. "I need you to trust me. Do you think you can?"

I tried not to blink, afraid the tears would roll down my face and never stop. I nodded. "Yes. I do."

He smiled at me like my answer was imperative to what he was going to say next. "Great. Listen to me when I say we will not be burying your friend anytime soon." I felt my heart squeeze. "Charlie, I know how much you love her, and because of that alone, I promise you that she'll stay on this side of the ground."

There was something in his words that made my gut loosen. He meant what he said, and because of that, I believed my friend would genuinely be all right.

The vampire said, "We need to go and secure the perimeter." The way he said it made it sound like it was a code word for something else entirely. I made a mental note to ask Jamison later what that was all about.

Jamison kissed me lightly on the top of my head before following my brother and the vampire out of the house.

Jolene sighed. "And so it all begins. No sense in fighting it. One by one, we will all eventually lose bachelorette-hood to love."

"Yep," Sammy nodded. "Definitely batty."

Tandi was in shock. "This might be my last night alive, and I'm more depressed over the fact that I didn't buy those cowgirl boots that cost an arm and a leg than I am over the loss of a possible future lover."

Jolene laughed. "Those must have been some boots."

Tandi wiped a tear from her eye. "They were. No more crying. Tonight, we'll party like rock stars. We'll eat

everything unhealthy that there is and not worry about calories or having to work out the next day."

Trying to make her laugh, I said, "Seriously? Tandi, you've never been on a diet in your entire life, unless you count that time you went on an all-fruit diet, but I don't think that counts because you coated everything in chocolate first. And the only time I ever got you to go to the gym with me, you drove us around the block for thirty minutes, waiting for a parking spot to open up closer to the gym entrance because you didn't want to walk far."

Tandi huffed. "Well, it's true that I would rather drink Mexican tap water than work out, but it's rude for you to point it out when I'm practically on my deathbed. And for the record, I know that I would be the first to die in The Hunger Games, not because I couldn't make a kill, but because all that running and hiding just wears me out thinking about it. I could accept death, as long as I have pie first."

"Ugh, people?" Sammy pointed at Jolene. "I think she's rechecked out of reality."

Jolene's beautiful pixie face looked around the room before her gaze settled on me. "I did it again, didn't I?"

Tandi, never being one for subtlety, said, "Yep, honey, you went around the bend, but you're back now, and that's all that matters."

Jolene gathered my warm hands in her cold ones, and the look in her eyes made heat travel up my back, causing sweat beads to form. "What is really isn't. You are going to be faced with so many choices. Don't try to decide your own fate. I've seen you throw out the welcome mat for death and long for its embrace. You have to fight the shadows, Charlie. Fight the temptation." She came out of whatever memory she was wrapped up in and leaned back against the cushions, her pretty face pale.

We all sat in silence for several minutes before I said, "That was really intense. So, uh, Jolene, do you have anything else to give me other than that…"

While I was trying to think of the right word, Tandi said, "Completely confusing and useless information?"

"Sorry. It comes in bursts, and sometimes I can't decipher what all the images mean. The vision wouldn't let me see that far. I'm sorry, Charlie. If only I was stronger, I could pick and choose what I wanted to see or deem helpful, but I'm not… there yet."

I gave her a watery smile. "It's okay. Thank you for telling me what you did."

"I'm not going to lie, snitches, this night blows," Tandi said.

We all nodded in agreement. Jamison had made a promise to me, and I had one of my own. I also promised myself that I wasn't about to lose my best friend. My friend with a heart of gold that thought if she could bring just a little laughter into the world with her commentary, she felt she had done her job. I refused to lose her. She would not die. Reaching over, I grabbed her hand and squeezed until her eyes met mine.

chapter twenty two

Since I had given my bed up for Jolene, I found myself later that night, being woken up on the living room floor. Someone was unzipping my sleeping bag. Rolling over, I saw Jamison crawling into my bag. "Can I lay with you?"

I scooted over and felt him meld his body to mine. Rolling over in his arms I tried to make out his face in the dark. I knew with his eyesight he had no problem seeing me. His hand cupped my chin and within in seconds he was biting my lower lip. I pushed on his chest with a moan before reprimanding him. "My brother is upstairs. Go to sleep."

He was chuckling as I rolled over in the tiny space that I was left with. He draped a massive arm over me, and I felt completely safe as I breathed in his warm scent, letting sleep claim me once again.

That night I dreamed. I dreamed of a place far away filled with horrors. A place that evil dwelled and was foreign to anything good. My sleep was pitiful, and I wasn't sure how many hours I had gotten before the commotion started. I was jostled awake when something the equivalent of a grenade went off outside, shaking the entire house. Poor Wes. We would need to move after all of the destruction that kept happening to our home.

Jamison rolled out of the sleeping bag, taking me with him. As I looked around, I saw everyone up and running in different directions, except for Jolene, who was on the couch rocking back and forth with her arms around her midsection, and Tandi, who was missing.

Wes strolled into the living room with nothing on but a pair of sweatpants hanging low on his hips. "There are ghouls circling our house."

Jamison opened the front door, and I tried to peer out before he shoved me back, slamming the door with a curse. Going to the window, I caught a glimpse of the flying creatures Wes must have been talking about. They flew on what looked like wooden sticks. They had clumps of stringy hair falling in front of their hideous faces. Patches of their skin appeared to be missing.

In shock, I asked, "What are they doing?"

"They're trying to keep us from leaving the house." Jamison pulled me away from the window. "Their skin is poisonous. No matter what, don't get close to them."

I had already decided to stay far away from those creatures but I nodded anyway. "Why do they want to keep us in?"

Wes, now fully clothed, said, "Because the demons will be here any second. They don't want us to be able to run and hide." He laughed. "They must not know me." Only my brother would find humor in a situation like this.

Wes walked over to the wall, pulling back one of the light fixtures. A secret door opened, revealing a room full of weapons. "Everyone help yourself."

How did I not know that was there? And when did he have time to do that?

Jamison let out a whistle. "You just went up a notch, Undertaker."

He started grabbing things: guns, knives, and a bow and arrow. He grabbed hold of me and strapped weapons onto my body, too.

"Do these things even work on demons?" I asked.

"They're not just normal weapons, love. They're enchanted with spells. You can feel the magic radiating off of them. Remember the only way to kill a demon is to take its head or rip out his heart, and we're not completely sure how much you can do before you tire out. You're not immortal," Jamison said. "Your wind will help hold them back, but just in case there are too many, these weapons can be your backup plan."

He handed me some sort of weapon resembling black stars with serrated edges.

"I don't know how to use these," I said.

Wes came over to me. "All you have to do is throw. One of the spells these weapons are enchanted with is the ability to always find its mark. Focus on what you want to hit. Aim and then release. The weapon will do the rest. What's cool about these shurikens is they're enchanted to come back to you like a boomerang."

Laden down with weapons, I asked, "Can't I just freeze time and take out the demons one at a time?"

Jamison's hand stilled on his bow and arrow as he thought. "I don't know if you can freeze large numbers of supernaturals. Or how long you can keep them that way. But it's worth a try. I would think it takes a lot of energy. Try not to weaken yourself to the point of exhaustion. This might be a long fight."

He had a point. "I need to go find Tandi."

Wes pointed towards the bathroom. "I passed her on her way to the bathroom."

Stephan ambled into the living room, looking like he was in between scenes on a movie set. Sammy was gently snoring, his chubby legs hanging over an armchair. Poor Jolene was still staring off into space.

"I'll go check on her." I started toward the guest bathroom, when the house was consumed with smoke. I staggered back toward Jamison. Demons were popping up everywhere. There were already fifteen in the living room, and more smoke was filtering in. Then, like a bad dream, François appeared in front of us.

Looking at Jamison, he said, "The Demon Prince said to kill the Prince of Wolves. In fact kill all of them, except the witch." He pointed a finger at me. "Oh, and Beautiful, the Demon Prince made sure there will be no time manipulation going on today. It cost us dearly, and we have to have you playing fairly." Before I could move, he blew orange powder into my face. Jamison had shouted something, but it was too late. As I wiped the remaining residue from my face, François had vanished.

"What did he just do to me?"

"He gave you some sort of drug." Stephan shook his head. "Then he ran. I guess he didn't want to get his hands dirty. Everyone is a coward nowadays. Have you noticed that?"

Jamison gave me a horrified look. "Go lock yourself upstairs."

There was no way that I was going to leave the people that mattered the most to me. He must have recognized the look I gave him because he let out a frustrated growl before he smashed his lips to mine for a quick kiss.

"Balls up!" Sammy sat up long enough to grab a blanket from the back of the chair. He covered his small body before he huffed, "If there is any way to move this fight outside, that would be great. I'm having a dream about the curvy blond, and I kind of want to get back to it."

"Dude," Jolene said, "Your familiar sucks."

"For real," I shouted to the lump in the chair. "Get up and help us. I just got powder to the face. I could be dying!"

"Relax," he said. "I need sleep, and you're not dying."

Jolene nodded. "Yep. Definitely sucks."

I couldn't wholeheartedly disagree at the moment, so I said nothing.

Jolene stood up. "I really don't want you to think I'm bailing on you, but Ariana said I had to be gone by six in the morning, and it's two minutes 'til. I'll see you around."

I watched from a window in horror as she stepped outside. The ghouls were circling above her. She shot them a bird as she walked right to her car with no incident. They completely ignored her. What. The. Hell?

"Tandi," I shouted. "Stay in the bathroom!" Then I heard an earth-shattering scream. I knew that set of lungs, but I couldn't see her. The whole house was filled with demons.

A demon charged at Wes, missing him by an inch and went careening into where Sammy was laying. Poor Sammy flew through the air crashing into a bookcase. He jumped to his feet, his little fist shaking. "Oh, you bugger! All I wanted was my beauty rest! That's it! You want my attention? Now you have it!"

Sammy pointed a finger at the demon. A lightning bolt shot from his fingertips as he zapped the demon. He kept pointing his finger, and the demon looked like a bug caught in a bug zapper. "What are you waitin' for, wolf boy? Take his head."

Jamison swung two short swords steadily as he moved through the crowd, taking heads as he went. "A little busy at the moment, little man."

A bolt of lightning flashed towards Jamison, and he swore as it hit him on the backside. Sammy shrugged. "Sorry, wolf, I missed."

"Cut it out Sammy," I said as I tried to call my wind to keep the demons at bay. Anger flared in me as nothing happened. I was completely helpless. My worry intensified immensely for my friends. I would not be able to help them in the slightest. "Well, at least we know what the powder was for. To dull my powers. I'm completely helpless."

"You're too strong for that potion to stay in your system for long," Sammy said. "Once it starts to wear off, use your ice, girl. Think about what you want to find. Their hearts! Then send the ice their way. Earn your keep."

Ugh. I was really wishing I could have chosen my familiar. The problem with the stars is if they were embedded in a demon's chest then they couldn't boomerang back to me. I was running out of weapons, but I continued to throw the stars that Wes let me borrow until I felt the edges of the drug starting to wear off. Poor François underestimated me once again. Once I felt more power flowing through my veins, I took Sammy's advice and sent my daggers made of ice to the object I wanted. The heart of whatever demon stood in front of me. My ice wasn't coming to me as quickly as it once had, but it was coming. I ignored my shaking hands. I was barely contributing, and I was already tired.

As I moved in the direction Tandi's scream had come from, Jamison snagged my arm, pulling me to a halt. I tried to wiggle from his grasp. "There's no way you can get through the throng of demons safely," he said. "We need to defeat the ones that are directly in our path. It'll only take us a little while to kill the whole lot. You have to be patient."

"Patient? Are you serious? My friend needs me."

He dodged a blow to the head before he swung his blade at the demon. "Then fight faster!"

Stephan was a blur as he went in between demons. He didn't bother with a weapon as he punched his hand through their chests, coming away with a heart. "I can make my way to her, but it'll take me a few minutes." I felt a surge of relief that the vampire was on our side.

Sammy whistled as he ran in between a pair of demon legs. He grabbed a weapon that was twice his size from the wall. How he would ever swing that blade without falling on his face was beyond me. But he did and with a certain amount of skill that was pretty impressive. Maybe I would keep him.

Wes's scythe was in his hand. The image he projected was enough to make the Devil himself shudder with fear. With a look of pure, deranged excitement, he jumped over the couch, yelling, "Come to Daddy!"

If only I could freeze time, I could get to my friend. I could tell my powers were nowhere close to freezing anyone yet. The sooner these demons were laid to rest, the sooner I could save Tandi. I was so busy focusing on the wall of demons in front of me that I let one slip up behind me. He grabbed me by my hair, jerking my neck back. I dipped my head under his arm, making his fist even tighter in my hair, but now I faced him. I put a hand on his chest and called wind to me. Air surged into him, and he was cleaved in two.

"Ha," Sammy shouted. "I told you! There's so much more to you, girl. Demons better watch out. My girl is back in business and looking for customers."

My knees were weak, that had required a lot of energy, but I refused to stop as I had a little bit more left in me and my friends needed me. I skirted around bodies with one goal in mind. To make sure Tandi lived.

chapter twenty three

amison killed demons like taking out pins in a bowling alley, but it seemed every time he dropped one, another popped back up in his place. Not even a bead of sweat was on his perfect face as he moved like a well-oiled machine. Without breaking stride, his movements changed, and I could see the beast beginning to swirl inside of him and wondered if anyone else noticed Jamison called on his true form to come out and play. The moment his eyes changed colors I knew the transformation was complete, and if I thought he was unbelievably powerful before, the beast made him unstoppable.

The vampire, Stephan, was lightning fast. He would be in one spot one second, then directly in front of a demon the next, ripping its heart out. My brother swung his scythe in a fluid motion, taking the heads of demons. I gave a mental eye roll at his eerie smile. It was hard to believe how much he was enjoying this, even if he was getting rid of evil. The power high he got from harvesting souls must be something else. Sammy had snuck around the demons to try and attack from behind. I knew he was still alive because every once in a while, I heard him giggle.

I was continually throwing ice like bullets, aiming for the heart to kill the demons, and when I felt tired I threw the stars, wounding and slowing the enemy down to make them an easier kill for the others, but we were not making much progress. The four immortals fighting at my side were graceful in their deathly blows, but I felt myself growing impatient. We were outnumbered two hundred to one, and my friend needed me.

"A little help," Sammy shouted as two demons had him backed in a corner. "Use your fire."

"My fire is useless on them."

"Humph." One demon picked Sammy up and threw him against the wall. "Wazzock! Send it like you do your ice, like you're trying to pitch for the major leagues. And hurry before they rip me to shreds."

I felt a burst of power come from within me just as a ball of fire hit the demon, sending him flying through the air. He burst into flames, leaving nothing but ash in his wake. I looked over at Jamison, who had stopped two feet from me with his mouth open.

Finally, he smiled that sexy half smile and said, "That was awesome."

He flipped his sword around and ran back into the throng of demons. I started aiming my palms at demons, alternating between ice and fire. Sweat dripped down into my eyes, and I was so tired I could barely stand, but I kept fighting. I wasn't immortal like the boys who fought beside me. All I had to carry me was my will.

After the fourth demon caught on fire, Wes yelled over the commotion, "You have got to be freakin' kidding me. How the hell am I supposed to get these burn marks out of the floors?"

Letting go of another ball of fire to take out the demon closest to my brother, I winced as the Persian carpet lit up. I shouted back so he could hear me, "I think it's time to sell this fixer-upper."

He never stopped fighting, but in between the kills, he said, "I don't think our insurance covers this type of fire."

Jamison was fighting a small group of demons, but another group crept up behind him for a surprise attack. I raised my hands, feeling the heat leave me in a rush. All four demons reeled in the air from the impact. They crashed through the front window, bursting into flames as they hit the lawn.

I heard Wes cursing. "Reign in your emotions, Charlie. You know he's immortal. You don't have to burn down the whole damn house trying to save him."

Jamison laughed. "I think it's cute you think I need saving, though."

I bit my lip, looking at the gaping hole where the window used to be. I knew an apology just wouldn't cut it. But the good news was the demons were starting to thin out. From the corner of my eye, I saw someone with long, blonde hair running through the kitchen. I yelled, "Tandi!"

I completely ignored that my gas tank was now close to empty as I released fire as I went. Scorching demons in a crimson tidal wave, I made a blazing path, so I could get to Tandi. I made it past Jamison, Wes, and Stephan, and even though I heard them screaming for me not to take another step, I kept going toward my friend. Just as I was closing in on Tandi, a demon appeared behind her, jerking her back by her hair. He held her in front of him like a shield.

I knew there were still traces of whatever François had given me pumping through my body. I also knew I was about done for the night. I might be able to freeze everyone once, but that would be it. My gut told me to hold off, but at the moment the demon tilted Tandi's head to a weird angle, I knew he was about to kill her.

There was no way in Hell I was going to let this demon murder my friend.

I drained the last of my power, freezing every being in this room. Knowing that I wouldn't be able to hold them for long, I quickly came up behind the demon and shoved my dagger through his heart. I was working on freeing Tandi from his clutches when time began ticking again.

In the distance, I heard Wes shout, "Duck!"

I wrapped my arms around Tandi and threw us to the ground. Wes's scythe came soaring above our heads, taking the demon's head off.

"Damn demons broke into the bathroom. All I had was a plunger and Lysol to defend myself. Just so you know even demons don't like anti-bacterial spray to face." Tandi groaned as I rolled off of her. "Wow, that was an intense moment."

"Yeah," I said as I looked over to where Jamison and Stephan were fighting the last of the demons. Within seconds, all the demons were dead. We were all tired and coated in demon blood, but we were alive. And that counted for something. "Whatever François gave me made me weak. I'm completely tapped out."

I helped Tandi stand to her feet. She dusted herself off as her nose wrinkled in disgust at the numerous demon bodies piled all around us. "It looks like the soothsayer was wrong. I survived this." Her shoulders lifted up in a small shrug.

Wes sauntered over to us. "We're not out of the clear yet. There is still an expiration date above your head, Tandi. Just be cautious."

The hair on the back of my neck stood up at his ominous words. Tandi wrapped her arms around her middle and her chin dropped to her chest. She started to move away from me, but I grabbed her arm and gave it a squeeze.

"You're going to be fine."

She gave me a little nod. Her eyes shone with unshed tears. "Sure."

Stephan gave a loud yawn as his eyes scanned the massive destruction that was once known as our beloved house. Killing a horde of demons must have bored him. "I think I'll go kill the ghouls circling the house. It's been at least a couple of weeks since I've seen their ugly faces."

Wes walked toward the front door. "Oh, they aren't going to be pretty, pretty boy. I'll help with the ghouls."

"There are only six of them," Stephan said.

Wes opened the door for the vampire. "Can't let you have all the fun, now can I?"

Sammy shook his head as he followed my brother and the vampire out the door. I knew that he wasn't going with them to help or even supervise, but more so he could make jokes at their expense. My familiar had a very dry sense of humor.

Jamison shook his head as he came over to me. He enfolded me in his arms, and I leaned into him. He felt like home. Warm and inviting. Tandi mumbled something under her breath as I heard her shuffling her feet away from us. He lowered his head and kissed each one of my eyelids before his lips touched mine. Yearning slammed through me. A burning urgent need that I've never felt or known before settles low in my abdomen. He pulls back with my name on his lips. His blue eyes show so much emotion that my knees almost buckle. Jamison stroked my back, and my mark tingled pleasantly under his hand. I was about to ask him to kiss me like that again when I heard a scream. We almost tripped over one another as we ran into the kitchen where François had Tandi entrapped in his arms five feet from us.

His beady eyes glared at me. "Leave with me now, and I will spare your friend. You will be a Demon Prince's queen and rule by his side. Never wanting for anything."

My powers were utterly drained. I tried to take a step towards my friend and François, but Jamison's arms tightened around me. "You know he has no intention of letting her go."

"You will be a queen! As we speak, he is preparing for your new home."

"I'm already a Queen. I don't need your Demon Prince. Let my friend go, and I promise I won't kill you for this."

François leered at me as he dragged Tandi towards the front door. "When grief overwhelms you, remember you could have saved her."

"Wait!" I screamed, but it was too late. François pushed Tandi out the front door. Jamison lunged for him, and they both disappeared around the corner of the house. A moment later, I heard the demon scream like a frightened little girl. It wasn't the demon's head rolling across my sneaker that made me feel faint. No, it was an entirely different image in front of me causing bile to rise in the back of my throat. There stood Tandi in between two ghouls, screaming, while they bit her. They were like piranhas. Her arms and face had scratches, but it was her neck that made me scream. A chunk of her flesh was missing. There was no doubt in my mind that a major artery had been pierced.

"Tandi!"

I was almost to her when Jamison caught me from behind. "It's too late, Charlie, the poison is already inside of her."

Sammy appeared in front of me, his little body doing its best to block me. Didn't he know that it was not me who needed protection? A piece of my heart was being torn apart by ghouls this very instant.

My knees hit the ground, and I started wailing. My heart felt like it was about to crumble as Jamison pulled an arrow from his quiver and let fly from his bow over and over again. Four ghouls had dropped to the ground where Wes and Stephan killed them the second they landed. The poison from the ghouls must not fatally harm vampires or the Undertaker because they weren't careful about dodging it.

The ghouls holding Tandi were trying to claw their way through her when Stephan tackled one of them to the ground. Rolling off the creature in one fluid motion, he hovered over the ghoul as he punched his hand through the hideous creature, ripping its heart out.

The remaining ghoul let out a shriek that would give me nightmares for the rest of my days. The creature threw what looked like a wooden spear at Tandi. I screamed as it went right through her stomach. She gripped the handle sticking out of her torso with a shocked expression on her face. Her chest heaved a couple of times, then she became very still, her eyes going blank.

My friend was dead.

chapter twenty four

Pulling on my hair, I screamed. How could this have happened? Jamison promised me that my friend would be okay. Somewhere through the fog, I saw Jamison killing the remaining ghoul by snapping its neck, but I took no satisfaction in that. I heard a sizzling sound from where his bare hands must have touched its poisonous skin. Wes came over to me, wrapping me in a tight hug. One that I didn't reciprocate or need. Stephan kneeled beside Tandi and rested his forehead in his hand, as if he was grieving, when it was my best friend lying there!

"We knew it might come to this," Stephan said.

Jamison cast me a glance before going to kneel on the other side of Tandi. "She knew it, too. What was the verdict?"

"She agreed wholeheartedly. I told her it was more of a curse than a blessing, and that most of my life, I wish I would have chosen death," Stephan said. "I've never really met anyone like her. She just patted my hand and said, 'Anything as hot as you shouldn't have worms crawling through empty eye sockets. And, to be honest, I'm kind of a big deal, too, you know?' But I really don't like the thought of having this beautiful creature end up with the same fate as me."

What the hell were they rambling about?

Wes cradled me in his arms. "I don't feel her soul, so you must have begun the transition last night. What are the final steps?"

That made me snap out of my grief. "What? What are you talking about? She's not dead?"

Jamison came to me. Squatting in front of me, he gently wiped away my tears. "It's almost impossible to cheat death once someone has been marked, so we called Ariana last night. She said this was Tandi's fate. That's where Stephan comes in. She said he was to give her some of his blood."

"So giving her Stephan's blood does what? Is she dead or is she not dead? And why did you not tell me this last night?"

"Ariana said if we told you, you would intervene. This is her fate."

I shrugged him off of me. "Of course, I would have intervened. Screw fate! My friend is dead."

"Ish," Stephan said. "Dead-ish."

Jamison started to reach for my hand again, but something in my face must have told him to stay back. I was ready to snap. How could he have known about this and not told me? "Stephan's blood buys us time. She had his blood in her when she died. If we act quickly, he can turn her."

My eyes widened with shock. "Turn her? Like into a vampire?"

"Your friend was going to die, Charlie. If you intervened, she would have still died, just in a different way." Jamison dropped his head. "I knew there would be a possibility you would hate me for this—"

"I don't hate any of you. Disappointed and pissed? Yes to both. Telling me this is the way it was supposed to be and I should throw all of my trust and faith into a soothsayer I have never met is beyond ludicrous. But as long as my best friend comes back, I'll take her any way I can get her."

Stephan cleared his throat. "There is more to it than her just becoming a vampire." Gently cradling Tandi's head in his lap, he said, "If she is not trained and closely watched for her first part of transitioning, she will have no control."

"What do you mean by control?" I asked.

Wes stood up, walking over to where Tandi lay. "He means that she might become like Jack the Ripper. Vampires have an unstoppable lust for blood. If they don't learn how to control it when first rising back up—"

"Then your friend will no longer be who you knew her to be," Jamison finished.

With a frustrated sigh, Stephan said, "I will have to train her if I sire her."

"But you don't want to sire her, do you?" I asked.

"No, not really," Stephan said, "but I can't let her die, either."

Blood poured out of the wound on Tandi's neck and stomach. Tears trailed down my face at the image that would be forever ingrained in my brain. "You will forever have my gratitude, Stephan, if you can bring her back to us."

"Funny that you should look at it like that. Hopefully, you will always remember this day, in case you realize that it is truly a curse I bestowed upon your loved one," Stephan said.

I shook my head. "No. It will never be a curse to us. Even if it does alter her personality. You've given her a second chance; one that she even asked for, correct?"

Stephan nodded. "Yes. But still—"

"But nothing. Do what it takes to bring her back to us," I said.

Stephan met my eyes. After a few seconds of hesitation, he bit into the flesh on his wrist. He was still gently cradling Tandi's head as he lowered his wrist to her mouth. I watched as blood dribbled down her chin and into the gaping hole in her chest. Nothing happened. Stephan must heal extremely quickly because he had to keep biting into his flesh. Finally on the third attempt, Tandi's eyes popped open. She grabbed Stephan's wrist, pulling it hard against her lips.

In a calming voice, he whispered, "Easy, gorgeous." Minutes went by before her eyes rolled to the back of her head and she passed out.

"Now what?" I asked Stephan.

He stood, lifting a sleeping Tandi in his arms and took her into the house. The rest of us followed. "Now, we wait. Soon, she will rise, and we will see how she handles the transition. I must warn you: some go crazy with the blood lust upon awakening and cannot control themselves. Some even decide they no longer want to go on as the undead and walk out into the sunlight to end their misery."

"No, not Tandi. She's made of tougher stuff than that."

"Let's hope so." Stopping at the guest bedroom, Stephan turned back to us. "I will take her in here to rest. When she wakes, I will come for you. You can say goodbye, and then we will leave."

Tears were streaking down my face. Since I was five years old I haven't been separated from my best friend.

Sammy, who had stood by silently the whole time, piped up, "I have a weird feeling about all of this. I can't quite put my finger on it, but I have a deep fear for your friend, and it has nothing to do with Tandi coming back as a vampire. Mind if I have a looksee at your mother's book?"

I nodded as I watched Stephan take Tandi into the bedroom and shut the door with his heel. I stared at the closed door, wondering if I would ever have my friend back, or just a fragment of the person I used to know. My heart was broken, but I refused to grieve for my friend when there was still hope. Hope that she would be the same girl that I had loved since kindergarten.

chapter twenty five

I sat on the couch, facing Jamison. My anger started to dwindle down from being convinced that everyone I trusted kept me out of the loop on purpose, to maybe I should try to understand their reasoning. "You believe that not telling me about Tandi was in her best interest?"

"Yes."

Truth.

"Do you believe she will still be the same? Or do you think that I have lost my friend forever?"

He took his time answering, carefully weighing his words. "I believe that the bond between you both is too strong for her to not overcome whatever hurdles that might separate you both in the future."

Again, my gut told me that he believed his words.

"Waiting for her to wake up is like waiting for water to boil. Distract me?"

He grabbed my legs and gave them a tug, causing my whole body to slide closer to him. I raised one eyebrow.

"Not the kind of distraction you're looking for, huh?"

I studied him. His blond hair was messy from the recent events, giving him a tousled look. His blue eyes twinkled with mischief, and I felt my heart flutter in my chest. At some point, I had fallen head over heels for this guy. What would I do when he decided to go home?

The back of his hand skimmed my cheek. "Hey, are you okay?"

I nodded, even though I wasn't entirely sure I was in fact okay. "Tell me something about your life."

His brow was furrowed like he knew something was off with me. Good luck trying to figure it out. I was just as confused.

"Your brother reminds me of my brother years ago. When I was little, my brother became my guardian just like your brother has become yours. Except he was a lot younger, and there was always some Degenerate trying to come after us or some exiled wolf who thought they could challenge us both to take our family's throne."

"Figuratively speaking or do you actually have a throne?"

For the first time, Jamison actually looked a little bashful. "Yeah, there's a throne and a crown that my brother never wears."

"You're embarrassed that you're a prince?" At his scowl, I laughed. "I find that unbelievable charming." He gently rubbed my feet, and my mark began to warm. "Hey, Jamison, this mark… Why does it always tingle?"

"There is something I've been meaning to tell you. I just didn't know how to begin—"

Stephan coughed from somewhere behind us, and Jamison's words were all but forgotten as Tandi came around the corner. My jaw hit the ground.

"Tandi?" I screeched, as I ran to her. She embraced me in a tight hug. "Is it really you?"

She giggled. "Yes, just a better version."

I scanned my friend from head to toe. She was completely healed. Her hair was the same color and length but now held more shine and luster. Her complexion was flawless, and her cat-like green eyes were a lighter shade. And her bod… wow.

"How are you feeling? Are you having second thoughts of, you know, becoming a vampire?"

Tandi, after pretending to think about it, finally said, "Yeah, no. I'm still alive. Well, not technically, but I've never really cared about technicalities. And did you check me out? I went from a size twelve to a four! I have collarbones. Jenny Craig couldn't touch this, baby." She pointed to her breasts. "And I get to keep the girls. I'm freakishly hot now, too, and I'm vain enough to say I prefer that over a beating heart."

"But the best part is you're completely healed."

"Yep, another plus." She tilted her head at Stephan. "Thanks to him."

I gave her another hug. "Well, I'm just glad to have my friend back."

Tandi gazed down at her feet. "About that… I have to go with Stephan to his retreat in the mountains. He says that if I don't go, there's a possibility I could go all psycho and start killing random people, and even though I'm like totally smokin' hot, I don't think I could live with myself if

I started eating people like popcorn out of a Cracker Jack box. That's just gross on so many levels."

I glanced over at Stephan, who was waiting patiently at the door. "You're taking her now?"

Solemnly, he said, "I'm afraid so. We must begin her training immediately."

"Well, when do I get to see her again?"

"As soon as she is in control over her blood lust," Stephan said.

"How long does that usually take?"

When the vamp didn't answer, Tandi grabbed hold of my hands in a show of unity. "Stephan, surely I'll get to see Charlie soon?"

When the room was deathly quiet, we both had our answer. I let out a quiet sob as tears rushed down her face. She gave me a wobbly smile. "Your brother hates goodbyes. I'm sure he is hiding upstairs." At my half shrug, she said, "Tell him goodbye for me and that I'll see him again soon."

Jamison stood up from the couch. He wrapped both of his arms around me—becoming my anchor. He gently kissed the top of my head before whispering, "Tandi has your number. She can call you anytime she wants or vice versa. And when he feels like she's not a danger—"

"She would never be a danger to me." I looked over at my best friend. "Right, Tandi?"

She currently had her eyes tightly squeezed shut, hunching over like she was in pain. Before I could ask what was wrong, Jamison put himself between me and Tandi, and Stephan grabbed Tandi by the elbow, leading her to the door.

I heard her whisper, "I can hear my best friend's blood pounding, and I wanted... I wanted to..."

"Shh, little one, I know. It's my fault. You should have woken up for the first time at my place. I knew better than to stay here," Stephan murmured against her hair. "We have to leave. All I can do is promise you that you will see your friend again when you have complete control."

Quietly, I said, "I love you, Tandi."

At the door, she hesitated. She turned toward me with tears in her eyes. "I love you, too. Forgive me?"

My smile wobbled. "For what? Alcoholics like alcohol. Witches like spells. Apparently, vampires like blood. I would be offended if my blood was a turnoff for you."

She gave a small laugh. "See you soon, friend."

I nodded, not trusting my voice to say goodbye.

Another pain must have hit her as she doubled over. Stephan whispered, "Sleep," in her ear, and Tandi went limp in his arms as he scooped her up and carried her out the door. As soon as I could no longer see them, I threw myself at Jamison. He clutched me to him as I soaked the front of his shirt with my tears. The day's events were catching up with me, and I was so unbelievably tired. I cried until there was nothing left of me. When I felt my body go slack with exhaustion, Jamison wrapped his strong arms around me. My head rested in the crook of his neck.

"What now?" I asked.

"You haven't lost your friend, sweetheart. She's a quick study with a great outlook on life. I promise you, it won't take her long to control her blood lust. You'll be back with her before you know it." He cradled me in his arms. "Your

brother's grown on me, but to be totally honest, I don't really want to stay here another moment. We have the key, and with the Demon Prince's infatuation with you, I would prefer not to wait around for his return. Why don't we leave this place?"

My heart pounded. He wanted me to go with him? He didn't want to leave me here in this town? "Where will we go?"

"Wherever you want. A Caribbean island? Somewhere warm and quiet. Or you can come back to my estate. Along the way, we can pop in and say hello to my brother. I would like for you to meet him." He tilted my chin up, so he could look me in the eyes. "There is something I've been meaning to tell you, but I didn't want to scare you."

Anxiety piled high in my stomach. "What?"

"Supernaturals have that one person that they are connected to. That person is called a mate. Most never find their mate; maybe they get impatient waiting for the 'one,' or maybe they don't live long enough to find their mate. Who knows? Ariana sent me here because she wanted me to find you. You're my mate."

Different emotions hit me all at once. I did my best to sort them out. I felt shocked, understanding, and… and relief. He was saying, "I know I should have told you as soon as I knew, but I was terrified I would lose you before I ever really had you, and—"

I threw my arms around his neck and peppered his face with kisses before I claimed his lips. Wrapping my legs around his hips, I leaned back to see his face. "Yes, I wish you would have told me, but I know that it would have freaked me out, so I get it. Being someone's mate is intense. I'm assuming it's not like marriage, where you can bow out if you have a disagreement?"

"Nope. Once we claim each other, it's for eternity."

"And the mark?" I asked. "It was never removable, was it?"

He winced a little. "The mark is the first step of three to claiming each other. It also allows me to find you wherever you go, and it tells other wolves that you belong to someone." He cleared his throat. "And as far as I know, it's not removable."

"What if I didn't want to belong to you?"

Hurt flashed across his face. "Then we would have asked Ariana if she knew of a way to remove the mark. Do you want it removed?"

"No. It's pleasant, and I have kind of grown attached to it, but that's not the point. I knew all along that you were hiding something. From here on out there will be no secrets among us. Agreed?"

"Of course."

I sighed in relief as his words rang true to my ears.

He barked out a laugh, crushing my body to his as he nuzzled my neck.

"We need to go. Get away from here. After I have you some place safe, I'll hunt down the Demon Prince to make sure he never has the chance to act out on his threat."

"Safe? I'm coming with you. He had a hand in hurting my friend. In fact, he was the mastermind behind the attack. It's my job to make him pay."

Jamison nuzzled my neck again. Must be a wolf thing. Whatever. I was digging it. "You're so vindictive. I like it.

Let's leave now. I'll buy you a suitcase full of clothes on the way to our destination."

"Oh, but I have to say goodbye to my brother, and I need to make sure that he is going to lay low somewhere, too."

Rolling his eyes, he placed me on my feet. "He's the Undertaker. You don't have to worry about him. Hurry. The sooner we get away from this place, the better."

Sammy would have to come with us. I mean, who else would he go with? But I decided to spring that tidbit of info on Jamison at the last minute. I ran up the stairs to my brother's bedroom. The door was open, so I didn't bother knocking. Wes was taking items out of a hidden safe and placing them in a small bag.

"What are you doing?" I asked.

"Packing my things. I just got off the phone with Ariana." He let out a sigh as he shoved items into his worn-out duffel bag. "I have to go after this Zombie Queen. Besides, you're leaving, aren't you?"

Feeling guilty, I said, "I had planned on it."

"I'm assuming he told you you're his mate?"

I was completely shocked. "How did you know?"

"I put the pieces together. I like him. He's a good fit. And he loves you. You can tell by the way he's always tracking you with his eyes. Plus, Ariana mentioned that you both were a walking Hallmark card." I had a feeling she didn't use those words. That sounded like a Wes interpretation. "Listen, I hate goodbyes. That's why I avoided going downstairs when Tandi was leaving. She's like my little sis, too, you know?"

"I know." I felt a lump form in my throat. Everything was changing. Constantly. I wouldn't be returning to school; my friend was going to be "adjusting" to her new self for a while, and now my brother was off on a mission. Part of me was sad, but the other part knew this was the way it was meant to be.

"I don't think the Demon Prince will come here, but I wouldn't put it past him. I hope after he sits and thinks about it, he'll come to the conclusion that no matter how many men he sends here, he'll never be able to wrangle the key, or you, from Jamison. At this point, he's probably going to go after the next key." Zipping his bag, he took one last look around his room. "I have to go steal a Vampire Princess slash Zombie Queen before she gets married. The bad news is ever since her engagement, she's been guarded by her mother's—the Vampire Queen's—army."

"Is there any good news?"

"Word has it that our little princess has been rebelling at every turn. I plan on stealing her right before her wedding and—"

"You're not going to kill her, though, right? Unless she absolutely deserves it. Like she eats small children for breakfast or something."

Laughing, he gave me a hug. "I'll let her live because you asked, but I'll let her know that if her diet doesn't meet your standards, I have permission to end her, which would be a hell of a lot easier for me."

"You never know, Brother, she might be a great person—an ally to our cause."

He gave me a look telling me he thought I was unbelievably naïve. "Yeah, and pigs fly."

"Maybe I'll get to meet her."

"I'm kidnapping her, not playing board games with her."

"Well, I think I'll still call you in a couple of weeks and see if I can come by to meet her."

Smiling, he gave me one final hug. "Only you would try and make a captive feel welcome. You'll probably bring apple cake, won't you?"

I batted my eyelashes. "Well, it is my best cake."

He tilted back his head, chuckling. He rubbed a hand over my head like I was a good puppy. "See ya, sis," he said, and tendrils of smoke wisped around him before he vanished completely.

I sat on his bed, looking around his room. Old posters still hung on the walls. The quilt that Mom had made him years ago was lovingly draped over an armchair. This house had been so much a part of me for so long, and now I planned on packing up and leaving. In my heart, I knew that Mom and Dad would approve of me getting out of this town. Especially if it was no longer safe. I know they would have adored Jamison, too.

Lost in thought, I didn't even have time to scream as the Demon Prince appeared in front of me. "Honey, I'm home," he snarled.

He blew the familiar powder in my face right before he hit me on the temple. He didn't bother trying to catch my limp form as it careened to the ground.

My last conscious thought was this demon didn't come back to this plane just to poison me. He was going to make me his slave, and I was ashamed that the coward in me wished that death would come for me first.

chapter twenty six

N umerous days later…

Another day had come and gone, and I was still locked away in this hellhole. Literally. My mind was starting to slip. At first, I was so sure it was shadows that came into my cell to torment me, but then as the days passed, I thought maybe I had just envisioned them due to lack of sleep and hunger. The mind could play tricks on you if you allowed it to, and I was too tired to try and decipher what was real and what was just a figment of my imagination.

As the days passed one into another, I had given up hope that I would be rescued. If it were a possibility, Jamison or my brother would have already done so. This feeling in the pit of my stomach was what it felt like when all hope was lost. There was a magical cuff on my leg that could not be clawed off. I knew because I had tried. The cuff suppressed all my powers and left me weak and useless. They couldn't have me freezing time, now could they? To think that not long ago, I had wanted a cure. A cure for whatever was wrong with me, and now I would give anything to have my powers back.

I had grown accustomed to the pain. Every day I was tortured—sometimes with fists and sometimes with whips—before being dragged out of my cell and thrown at the feet of the Demon Prince. And every day, he asked me the same question.

"Have you decided to accept your fate today and become mine?" He wanted me to rule by his side, and his fascination with the Queen of Witches and Warlocks was the only thing keeping him from killing me. He had already given up hope on the key and had explained to me his focus would now be on the other keys. They were easier to obtain, and, well, with me by his side…

But my answer was always the same. "No."

Someone came into my cell once a day with a small portion of food and water, and that was the only time I was allowed to eat or drink. My bones poked through my skin, and yet I could not bring myself to say yes.

Yesterday or the day before—I couldn't remember, as all the days seemed to run together—one of the guards had tried to get overly friendly with me and when he stepped close enough, I pulled his knife from its sheath and made a weak attempt at stabbing him. He laughed at my poor attempt, but not before he turned the knife on me, slitting my side. The wound was deep, and I prayed that it would get infected and kill me quickly, but I wasn't even blessed with so much as a fever. I also had a feeling that the Demon Prince would heal my wound before it killed me. Nonetheless, I didn't see the same guard again. There was a rumor that the Demon Prince had disposed of him. They could harm the mortal girl, but not fatally so. Apparently, the guard had made a mistake.

My cell door opened, and I cringed as I saw the whip dangling from my new guard's hand. The first time I had been whipped, I bit back the screams. They would not see me cry, but by the fourth day, the tears had flowed down my cheeks like a wet balm to my soul. They tried to break me, but I would not say yes.

The guard barked an order for me to stand. The hell with him. If he wanted to beat me, he could do it with me lying on the floor. I didn't have the energy and without my power, the only thing I had going for me was my stubbornness.

That's exactly what he did—beat me where I lay. I covered my face just in the nick of time. The whip hit me on my wrist. I pulled my knees up to my chest and made a tight ball, praying I was protecting all the important parts. If the guards hit me in the face, a healer would be sent in but anything else would have to heal on its own. The second hit of the whip stole my breath. My ribs felt like they cracked under the sting of the whip. By the third hit, my vision began to blur. I didn't remember anything after the fourth crack. I had blissfully passed out. Losing consciousness seemed to be my saving grace recently.

The hunger pains woke me. When those hit, I thought of Tandi and how she might be adjusting to her new life, hoping her own hunger pains were not too much for her.

More days passed. I was on a hamster wheel. Unable to get off. It was the same thing every day. Torture and denying the prince of demons. Night was different. At night when the shadows danced against the wall, I imagined my brother had won the heart of the vampire princess, and she had been drafted to our side… the Lux's side, and every new person brought to our side was one more gift to turn the tide in our favor. A big "screw you" to the Demon Princes of the world. When I felt like my mind was going to break, I daydreamed that Jamison searched everywhere for me, missing me with every beat of his heart. My mark no longer heated up. No longer brought me any joy and because of that, I knew my dreams were false. Did Jamison try to find me? Maybe and maybe he died for it.

The Demon Prince grew more impatient as I maintained my stubbornness. He was no longer overly concerned with my mistreatment. He requested that my next beating be in front of all of his council and underlings. They laughed and cheered at every crack of the whip. I wished, not for the first time, that death would claim me. After that beating, they had to drag me by my ankles back to my cell. My wet back left a trail of blood on the cold floor. I couldn't help but smile. My chances for infection grew every day, and maybe soon this would all be over.

That night they came for me again, which was rare. I was released from my cell once a day, to give the demon prince my answer and then for my nightly whipping. If the guards were feeling extremely lazy, they would let me remain in my cell while they tortured me. That way they didn't have to carry me back. Lazy asses.

But tonight was different. The way my luck had been going, different was probably a bad thing. The guards graced me with their presence again as they escorted me out of my cell. They took me in a different direction than I had ever been before. Maybe I could escape. All hopes of dying left me when numerous sirens surrounded me with yards of fabric and tools of the trade. The sirens were beautiful, their hair long and shiny. Obviously, they hadn't been beaten in a while. Snitches. Their ample bodies moved with grace and confidence. None of them would make eye contact with me. I begged them for help and they ignored me. They forced me into a bath, scrubbing every inch of me.

I almost vomited when their hands touched my wounds. Somehow, I managed to keep the bile down. There was no humility left for me to give them. After I was spotless, they dressed me in the finest fabric I had ever seen. A siren draped it over my bony frame in a Grecian style and clipped the fabric into place at my shoulders with rare jewels. Someone pushed me into a seat and started decorating my eyes with a heavy hand while another pulled and tugged on my hair. My arms were adorned with golden cuffs, and my fingers were weighed down with numerous rings. A ruby ring was placed on my left ring finger, and then I was shoved in front of a full-length mirror.

The girl reflected before me was not just beautiful, but striking as well, with her dainty features and violet eyes. She looked like a princess, even if she was too thin, but she wasn't me. The girl in the mirror died weeks ago and whatever fate they had planned for me, I was sure to sabotage because it would be a cold day down here in Hell before I said yes to the Demon Prince.

As soon as I was deemed perfect, I was led through a hall and into a room fit for a king. Inside the onyx tiled room, I was ordered to stand in the circle and wait for the Demon Prince to appear.

Demons of all sizes stood along the walls of the room. Torches hung from the walls. The flame cast dancing shadows of tiny demons. Thirty minutes I stood there, ignoring the smirks sent my way and the looks of pure hatred. I stood on weakened legs with my chin held high until the Demon Prince swooped into the room in his human form. Bile rose in my throat as he turned to me. Oh, Lord, no! It was Jamison's face looking back at me, but the man didn't have any of Jamison's swagger as he claimed his throne.

No. Oh, please, no.

Jamison's face smiled at me. "Want to take a guess at how I got this body, my little dove?" My mouth opened, but no words came out. "Have I rendered you speechless? Let me enlighten you. Your lover broke into my realm and killed several of my best demons. Demons that are not hard to replace, but still. When he was finally captured, I made him a deal. Would you like to know what it was?"

No, I didn't want to know. I wanted my heart to stop beating and for me to not take another breath, but that was not in the fates. Hands clenched, I said, "Why don't you do us both a favor and cut to the chase? I'm dying to get back to my cell."

He stroked a hand down his velvet jacket, something so unlike what Jamison would do. I wanted to cry. "After showing him that you were on death's door, he practically begged me to overtake his body on the condition that I give you a life of luxury from here on out."

My lips trembled at the thought of what Jamison had done. He'd sacrificed himself just so that I could live. Didn't he know that I would rather die a thousand deaths than live a grand life here, married to the Prince of Demons? There was no spell that could reverse what he had done. If I ever got a chance to kill the Demon Prince, I would be inadvertently killing Jamison, as well.

"So, I've brought you here tonight to ask you the same question that I did this morning—"

"No."

It might have been Jamison's eyes, but it was the Demon Prince staring at me in shock. "Aren't you at least going to let me finish asking the question?"

With jerky motions, I took the ring off my finger and slung it across the marble floor, where it skidded to a stop at his feet. "No. My answer is no. Tonight. Tomorrow. A year from now. No." I took off each piece of jewelry and smiled as they hit the floor with a clanging sound. "Kill me now, Prince of Demons, because I will never marry you. I will never rule by your side. I prefer death over waking up next to you every morning."

He knew something I didn't. I could tell by the way his eyes twinkled, and his mouth fought a smile. For some reason, I believed I just played into the palm of his hand.

"And here I thought you would take comfort in at least seeing your lover's face every day and night. Hmm. Maybe I should dispose of this body and take another." I didn't respond. "It's interesting that you mentioned death. My sources say that the Reaper is in trouble of his own and unaware you have been missing for the last five weeks. He must have assumed you were safe with the wolf. You know what they say about assumptions," he said, chuckling. "I brought you a gift… an early wedding present, if you will."

He snapped his fingers, and a demon brought out a small bloody heap to the center of the floor, chucking it at my feet. The lump moaned and rolled over, saying my name.

"Sammy? Is that you?" I asked, kneeling beside him.

The demon prince gave me a wicked smile. "He is a bit unrecognizable, isn't he? Apologies. He put up quite a fight when we captured him, along with the wolf. I would like for you to ask yourself a question. Is denying me marriage worth his life? If the answer is yes, then he will become my slave, and every day he will feel death breathing on his neck just to escape it by an inch, so that he can relive it again the next day… And as for you, I will have someone drag you back to your cell, where you may or may not be lucky enough to die. If the answer is no, then let's take our vows now, and I will swear you will never want for anything, and not only will I allow this creature to live, but he can be your companion, free to roam my castle for as long as you allow him to."

I gathered Sammy into my arms. The ivory of my dress quickly became covered with his blood. My tears dropped onto his bruised face. I ran a shaky hand over his whitish-blond hair, caked with blood. "If you vow to never harm him again, then my answer is yes."

Something inside of me broke with those words. It was the snap of the final straw. What other option did I have? It was perfectly acceptable in my book to will myself to die when I had no one else to think of, but how could I cast Sammy, my mother's gift to me, to a fate that was worse than death?

"You have my vow. No more harm will come to your friend, and he will live a life of luxury, just like you, until you will it no more."

At my nod, he walked to me. With a snap of his fingers, someone took Sammy from my arms. The Demon Prince gave orders that he be put in our chambers. If I had anything in my stomach other than bile, it would have hit the floor. Gripping me by my arms, he pulled me to my feet before giving me a forced kiss.

I would never have a future with Jamison. My heart cracked at the thought. He was gone. My heart shattered with the realization. My previous life was gone. I couldn't breathe. This was my fate. I was nothing but a shell. This was my future. Please don't let it be a long one.

The Demon Prince swatted me on my bottom and that's when I checked out.

Vows were chanted, a dagger was produced, and when I felt it bite into my skin, I didn't even flinch. Charlie had disappeared somewhere, and I had a hopeful feeling she would never be found.

chapter twenty seven

*A*fter hours of feasting, the party came to a stop. I had dreams of food like this, and yet I hadn't touched a bite. As the Demon Prince escorted me back to our room, I didn't bother taking in any of the scenery. To observe meant I was still here, and there was nothing left of me but a shell.

As he led me into the bedroom, I decided that if he got close enough to me while wearing that dagger of his, I was going to drive it through his heart. Then I would find a way to decapitate him.

Hope was a terrible thing.

He locked the door, and I spun around to face him. "Calm yourself, love."

"I am not your love."

"Yes, yes, you are. I knew it from the first time I laid eyes on you. You have all of my heart, so be careful what you do with it."

I snorted. "You owning a heart? What a joke."

He walked over to a settee, and I noticed Sammy was lying there with a half-smile on his face. Obviously, he had been hit so hard that he didn't know how dire our situation was, but if Sammy was in here, maybe he didn't plan on consummating the marriage unless...

"You promised not to hurt him," I spat.

The Demon Prince sat beside Sammy, placing a hand on his chest. Slowly, all of Sammy's bruises and cuts began to fade. Within minutes, Sammy was sitting up and swinging his feet back and forth an inch above the ground.

"You really knocked me around."

The Demon Prince smiled. "Had to make it look real, didn't I?"

No. It couldn't be.

I felt dizzy. "What's going on?"

The Demon Prince stood to face me. "It really is me, Charlie." I took a step back until my legs bumped into the bed, stopping my retreat. "It was the only way that I could get to you and bypass the thousands of demons making up the Prince's court."

"What kind of trick is this? You are not Jamison."

His blue eyes pleaded with mine. "You promised me a plane ride to a sunny destination, and then you disappeared on me, and I couldn't get to you quickly enough. When I couldn't smell your scent in the house anymore, I knew you were gone, and like a fool, I didn't ask for backup. I didn't even tell a soul where I was going." Sammy nodded. "This one woke to my shouts and trailed after me. I was too maddened to insist he stay behind. After I entered Hell, I had to go through one realm after another. Each battle was longer than the previous one, and all the while, I knew that every second I was away from you was one more second that you were here… with the Demon Prince."

My eyes shifted to Sammy. He was smiling and nodding at me. I looked back at Jamison. "It's really you?"

"Yes, love."

His arms opened, and I ran to them. I was scared this was another hallucination, so I clung to him while it lasted. He murmured soft words into my ear as he picked me up, cradling me like a small child.

"Shh, don't cry anymore, love. We must get out of here. We have perhaps twelve hours before anyone realizes that I'm a prince, just not the right one."

"Where is the Demon Prince?" I asked.

Jamison winced. "In the closet?"

My eyes darted around. "What?" I looked at the door Jamison was pointing at. "He's dead, right?"

"No. The closet is rigged, though, so whoever opens the door will cause an explosion. This whole room will be decimated."

"I'm guessing there is a reason he's still alive?"

"Yep," Sammy said, "as one of the royals, his death will be felt by all. Including his sister, Carmen. The reigning Queen of Hell." He rubbed his round belly. "I hope your blonde friend doesn't expect me to wait forever on her while she's trying to get her fang diploma. I mean, I'm a hot commodity, and you know who else is smokin' hot? The new queen. I could send her a gift basket congratulating her on her new title."

Congratulating her on her father's death? I had nothing to say to that. Apparently, neither did Jamison. Shaking his head, Jamison said, "Yeah, so the Queen of

Demons will not like that someone broke into this realm without permission and killed her brother. Keeping the Demon Prince alive a little longer is advantageous to us." He sat me down on the bed. "We need to leave right now, though. Sammy can remove your cuff. I'm going to heal you as much as I can, and then we'll fight our way out of here."

"Cut this cuff off of me and let's go."

He gave me a wide smile. "That's my girl, and Charlie, I'm sorry it took me so long to get to you."

I cupped his face in my hands. On closer inspection, Jamison appeared like a crazed man. His eyes were bloodshot, and he looked like he hadn't slept in days. The last thing I needed to do right now was wallow in self-pity or tell him the horrors I'd went through. Every day he spent trying to get to me was probably a horror of his own. "Don't worry about it. I had loads of alone time. Lots of self-reflection, which is good for the soul."

His laugh rumbled all the way from his chest. He knew I was lying through my teeth, but he appreciated my humor. His eyes were shiny as he pulled me to him one more time. The way he kept touching me told me it was hard for him to believe it really was me standing in front of him. The feeling was mutual. Jamison moved to the side, so Sammy could remove my cuff. He placed his chubby hands around the metal and said some words. The cuff heated up before it broke in two. My body immediately felt different, as if I was getting oxygen for the first time. Jamison set out to heal me. He couldn't put any of the weight I had lost back on my bones, but my cuts and bruises were long gone. He picked me up in his arms. "I wish I could give you more time but I can't. Are you ready?"

"More than ready," I say but my words are different than my body language. I was shaking from head to toe. Too much had happened and I feared I was going into shock.

"Hey, look at me, love." I stared up into his heavenly features. He gave me a slight smile before his mouth covered mine. His warmth, his love seeps into me as I press up against him. Sammy clears his throat as I shyly pull away from the one person who can keep me grounded.

"Let's get out of here."

He smiled at me with pride before he looked at Sammy. "It will be harder leaving than it was getting here, and we have more to lose on our return."

"Geez," Sammy said, rolling his eyes. "What am I, chopped liver?"

Each realm was exactly the same as far as atmosphere goes. Sammy said that each level was made up of layers of cavern walls. The floor was almost as slick as it was black. Cool to the touch like lava that had hardened over time. The only thing different about the realms was they were controlled by a different under lord. The under lords were in charge of their sections, only answering to the Demon Princess and Prince. Our goal was to skirt on the outside of each realm, where the outcast demons mostly resided. Apparently, each under lord had a lavish place in the center of each level, which made it easier on us.

There were twelve realms above us we needed to get through. The realm we had just exited was a piece of cake because everyone thought it was the Demon Prince leading us. But the next realm was tricky because those demons were considered the 'commoners' of the demon world. They looked at Jamison with suspicion because if he truly was the Demon Prince why would he be walking through the realms instead of just 'appearing' where he needed to go. We made it halfway through the realm before the first incident. We stumbled upon sixteen demons who knew we weren't where we belonged. I was extremely tired and my energy was low but I couldn't let Jamison and Sammy fight without contributing. I made tunnels of fog around the demons. Jamison and Sammy knew exactly where to find the demons but the demons didn't know where my boys were. It was perfect. Until the last demon somehow managed to work his way out of my fog. He scampered off before we could stop him. I assumed that he would report us to his under lord who would then report us to his boss the Demon Prince. Then all hell would break loose.

We hurried our pace. After we climbed through the second realm, Sammy explained that getting to me was tricky for them because they had to navigate through the realms, for the first time, as they had never had a reason to break into Hell. But he said our return wouldn't take as long, now that they both knew the way to go. I imagined we would have been out of this place sooner if it weren't for us having to fight our way out occasionally.

For the most part, we were able to avoid the demons, but sometimes they were blocking our exit, and the confrontation was unavoidable. Even though there were a ton of demons patrolling the boundaries, we still did our best not to be seen. Sometimes it was unavoidable. The 'unavoidables' is what was wearing me out. We came upon three demons, and my energy was depleted. Gone. Nothing. Nada. Not even a spark of fire. I watched as Jamison grabbed one demon by the throat slamming him into the demon behind him. Sammy was a blur as he jumped on their chests, taking out their hearts with a wicked blade he had found on a wounded demon a while back, while Jamison dealt with the third. My familiar was jumping up and down. "I haven't had this much action in ages, I tell ya." He hitched his chubby chin towards Jamison. "Blondie over there is a man on a mission. All he needs is some theme music."

Jamison was hiding a smile. My familiar had bonded with Jamison while I was gone. They made me happy. I really wanted them to like each other. Sammy had grown on me and Jamison, well, he was like my anchor in a storm. He made me feel rooted. We did our best hiding the bodies hoping it would buy us more time. Jamison took any food and ale that the demons had on them but it wasn't enough for all of us. I had a sickening feeling that he was giving me more than my fair share when it came to the looted goods. I could tell that the weight I've lost down here bothered him. Many times, I caught him staring at me with concern. He was almost taking it personally. Like it was his fault that I refused to eat while I was trapped here. It worried me. Jamison was a big guy–he needed more food to sustain him than I did. After nine days, we were hungry and tired, and barely in the fourth realm, when a power washed over us.

"That would be the Queen of Demons. She's letting everyone know something has happened to her brother. Time is of the essence now. We need to move fast," Jamison said.

We no longer tried to be quiet, moving almost in a blur. It was unheard of that an under Demon Prince died, and in his own court at that. We were on borrowed time. Soon, the under lords would be sending out patrols to ensure the same fate would not happen to them. That was when an idea came to me.

"I haven't used any of my powers in two days. I'm still tired, but I feel a little better."

Jamison gave me a weary look. "What are you thinking?"

"If you could tell me the way I could freeze time and carry you both on my wind for a bit. It would get us past the demons patrolling."

Jamison paced in front of me. It was clear that he didn't like my idea. His face was covered with doubt. Sammy cuffed him on the leg. "Listen, boy-o. I don't want her depleted of energy either, but the patrols are getting larger in numbers. Maybe she could at least get us pass this border patrol and the next."

Finally, Jamison gave me a nod. "I'm sorry."

"For what?"

He looked at the ground both of his hands in fists. I walked over to him placing my hands on either side of his face. "You have no reason to apologize. None of this is your fault. Do you hear me?"

He pulled me towards him resting his forehead on top of my head. He took a couple of deep breaths. "When we are out of here I'm never taking my eyes off of you again."

I gave a little laugh until I realized he was deadly serious. He was squeezing me so tightly. I realized in that moment that whatever I've recently endured might not have compared to the hell Jamison had been going through and some part of him holds himself accountable. I could feel his anguish.

I stepped back. "I'm going to freeze time and get us through on my wind, okay?"

With his nod, I did just that. I continued freezing time off and on for the next several realms until I had no more energy. We were on our last realm before we could claim freedom when the Queen of Demons showed up. She was maybe four feet tall, pudgy with a ruddy complexion, and was currently blocking our exit.

"Carmen?" Sammy said. "What kind of body have you snatched now?"

She flipped her ratty black hair behind her. "My asshat of a father sealed my body off, so I couldn't claim it. Apparently, he was trying to teach me a lesson. One that I never learned. Now, I'm left jumping bodies until I find mine. Total bummer."

This was the freaking Queen of Demons? A girl that said "bummer" and acted like a teenager who just got her cell phone taken away from her instead of her body. Wasn't expecting that.

"Introduce me to your friends, Sammy."

Sammy was still looking perturbed by the queen's body choice, which was more than a little hypocritical, considering Sammy looked like a shorter, hairy version of the Michelin man.

"Oh, yeah, sorry. Carmen, this here is the Prince of Wolves, and this is the Queen of Warlocks and Witches."

The Queen of Demon's pudgy cheeks lifted in a smile. "Cool. Nice to meet you. So here's the thing. I'm guessing one of you killed my brother? Apparently, he was just blown to smithereens in his own quarters. Personally, I'm not going to cry over it. He was a complete douche canoe, but since I've taken over for Daddy dearest, there has been some rebellion. You know how that goes. I have been ruling with an iron hand, putting heads on spikes. Doing the normal everyday ruler of the realms stuff, just to get a little respect. So now, I have to find the killers of my brother, make an example out of them, and yada, yada, yada, so that the other under lords feel safe and all that bull crap. The crown is heavy, but someone has to wear it." She tried to put a piece of hair behind her ear, and her fingers got caught in the tangled mess. "Ugh. This poor creature didn't know proper hygiene if it would have bitten her on the ass."

Jamison crossed his arms over his broad chest. "Example or not, we are leaving here. If you want to keep that crown on your head, I suggest you let us pass."

Her dull brown eyes widened. "Whoa! Temper, temper. You're not nearly as pleasant as your brother."

"You know my brother?"

"Duh." She pointed to the large demon army behind her. "As you might have noticed, I made it so they can't hear anything we're talking about. There are so many traitors. Who's a girl to trust? Maybe I should make more spikes for their heads." She held up a hand. "So not your problem. I get it. So back to your problem. You've killed my brother. I need retribution. But I also don't need the deaths of royalty on my hands, so let's negotiate. Shall we?"

"What is it that you want?" I asked, knowing she was going to open her mouth and say the key. There was no way I was letting Jamison give her the key. We worked too hard to have it.

"I'll let you pass if you vow to have Ariana contact me."

Shock colored Jamison's face. "That is what you would ask of me?"

"Yes, handsome. That woman promised me she would be sending a boy that was capable of helping me get my original body back, and I haven't seen him yet. I'm growing impatient."

Jamison looked at me with a question in his eyes. I gave him a shrug. This whole thing was off the charts crazy. I didn't know what I expected from the Queen, but this wasn't it.

"I vow to have Ariana contact you if you let us pass," he said.

The Queen of Demons nodded. "I will tell everyone the three of you were invited here by me personally. Then I'll blame Metrapho. He'll be your scapegoat. I've heard that he has been hurting small children again. He deserves to have his head spiked."

Sammy rubbed his chin. "Do you scream 'off with their heads' when this gruesome act takes place?"

She laughed. "No! But I should. That's hilarious." She pointed towards the exit. "Now, go and keep your promise."

With a wave of her hand, she pushed the fifty demons standing behind her up against the cavern wall. The Queen had skills. I nodded to her as we passed, but I didn't fully breathe until the sun was shining down on my face. I didn't fully laugh until we were miles away from the portal that led to Hell.

chapter twenty eight

U pon our return, Jamison told me what his plans were for the key and asked me what I thought. He was treating me like an equal. As if it was our key to protect not just his, and my heart swelled with love. He said, and I had to agree, that we needed to split up the key into two parts, making it more difficult to steal, but we also had to have quick access to it if we ever had a reason to use it. I thought his idea was fantastic.

We took half of the key to a pond behind Jamison's large estate. He told me a story that happened long ago. One where he rescued a family of water fairies from a shapeshifter that had the ability to turn into a sea serpent. Supposedly, the water fairies felt indebted to him and insisted in following him home. The tiny creatures resided in a bird feeder until Jamison realized they really weren't going to leave him alone, so he built a man-made pond just for them. I was in love with a powerful Prince of Wolves who had a heart of gold. I felt like I had won the lottery.

The family of water fairies consisted of the two parents that had three teenagers and according to Jamison, "the

cutest little toddler ever" named Marianna. Jamison called the father's name a couple of times, and we sat on the edge of the lake, waiting for the family of six to come up to the surface. I was beyond exhausted. My eyes felt like they had so much crust in them and all I really wanted was a bed, but when Marianna swam to the surface, even I had to smile.

Jamison was right; she was a beauty. She was maybe four inches tall and had the most beautiful head of hair I'd ever seen. Little blond curls hung all around her tiny shoulders. Her purple eyes studied me as she sucked on her little thumb. She was making her mind up if she liked me or not when the other family members swam to the surface.

The three boys looked identical. I was assuming they were triplets. All had dark brown hair and purple eyes. They favored their mother who curtsied when she saw me, causing me to smile even wider. When he introduced me to them, they all nodded shyly. Except for the boys, they wiggled their eyebrows at me and punched each other in the arms. I gave each of them a smile in return.

Marianna resembled her father, who was saying, "Sir, did you call us?"

"Yes, I did. I have a very important job for you and your family, Javann. It could possibly be dangerous if anyone ever found out what you were guarding, but do you think you and your family are up for the task?"

Javann looked over to his wife, who gave him an encouraging smile. "Yes, sir. We owe you our lives. In return we would guard whatever you wish us to with our lives."

Jamison was trying hard to hide a smile and failing. "I don't think it will put you in danger as long as you never speak of it to anyone."

Javann thought for a second. "I understand, sir. What will be guarding?"

Jamison gave him half of the key. There was no need to explain what it did or how important it was. The triplet's eyes were practically bulging from their sockets.

Javann held the key that was wider than he was. "Sir, you honor us with this task. To guard something so important." Javann's wife was wiping tears away and sniffling. "There are no words to tell you how honored we are."

"Thank you, friend. Hide it well. Now that that is out of the way, is there anything you or your family need?"

Whatever Javann was about to say died on his lips, as one of the teenagers said, "More trout? Oh, and maybe a water slide. That would be totally wicked."

Javann and his wife started chastising the young boy and his brothers who were now begging. Jamison laughed. "Absolutely. I've been meaning to build a dock now for a while. I'll get on that this weekend. I'll order a slide and a water trampoline. Those have always looked like a lot of fun."

The boys were jumping up and down with excitement while Marianna was still sucking on her thumb, trying to figure out if she liked me. Finally, she gave me a shy smile. That one smile made me feel like I had just won an Olympic medal.

"If you all will excuse us, Charlie needs sleep."

For whatever reason, my face blushed at his wink. He made the word sleep sound scandalous. Jamison helped me stand to my feet as we said goodbye to the water fairies. The teenager who had proved to be the most brazen stopped right before diving back into the water. "Oh, Mr. J?"

"Yes?" Jamison replied.

"Way to go; she's totally hot."

Jamison was laughing as the teenager disappeared into the water. We walked into his massive log cabin home as he spun me around, giving me a gentle kiss. "You are totally hot. Hopefully, the horny teenage water fairies won't steal you away."

I shoved at his chest. "You're so not funny. Just stop."

A yawn escaped before I could stop it. Jamison swung me up into his arms. "You need to sleep. I can't have a tired mate."

I curled my head against his chest and closed my eyes. The last thing I remembered was the steady beat of his heart and how I finally felt safe.

Four days and nights went by before I woke. My body was sore, but I was alive.

"You're awake."

Glancing over to my right, I saw Jamison slumped in a chair that was too small for his large frame. He looked

like he hadn't bathed or eaten in days, but he was still handsome.

My voice squeaked, "Hi."

He jumped up and got me some water. Putting a hand behind my head, he held me up while I drank.

"I'm still in shock that you came after me," I said. "You saved me."

"Of course I came after you. I told you once before I'll always come for you."

"I've been out for a while?" At his nod, I said, "I've never been so tired."

"You can't ever leave me again." Sitting down on the edge of the bed next to me, he took time gathering his words. "I love you with all my heart. When the Demon Prince took you, I almost went insane. It's going to be a while before I can let you out of my sight. Be patient with me?"

"You rescued me from Hell. I think I can be a little patient. You said that there were more steps in becoming your mate?" At his nod, I said, "I would like to complete the bond."

His blue eyes rounded in shock. "You are sure?"

"Absolutely sure. I want to be your mate."

He leaned down and kissed my forehead.

"Wait until I tell Tandi that I have a mate that would literally go to Hell and back for me. She is going to be so jelly." I sat up, stretching. "What are we going to do with the other half of the key?"

"I have a fireproof safe in the basement. It's hidden in a secret room. I think between the Prince of Wolves and the Queen of Warlocks and Witches, the two of us can keep it safe. Don't you?"

"Hell, yeah, I do."

Laughing, he scooped me up. "Come on, mate."

"Where are you taking me?"

"Before we complete the ceremony, you are in need of a bath. And since you're so weak, I'll have to bathe you myself."

I was too tired to blush. "Then will you carry me around and let me see your awesome house?"

"Your wish is my command. The only place I will not take you is the guest apartment. Sammy's made himself a home there and has got acquainted with Xbox. If we go there, he'll persuade you to play, and we'll be stuck there for hours, and I have different plans for you."

I giggled as he shut the bathroom door with his foot, and I realized that if a hot angel placed his hands on you every chance he got and carried you like you were the most priceless gift in the world, then the cliché was true. Love conquered all. I had a feeling that we had not fought our last battle against evil, but this man carrying me would make every fight worth winning, just so that I could say I belonged to him. This was a fate I could live with.

For the first time, I was waving my freak flag without worrying about the repercussions, and finally I felt like I wasn't pretending to be someone else.

Brandi Elledge lives in the South, where even the simplest words are at least four syllables.

She has a husband that she refuses to upgrade...because let's face it he is pretty awesome, and two beautiful children that are the light of her life.

24310264R00168

Printed in Great Britain
by Amazon